"Let's quit playing games, shall we?" Ellis told her.

It was not a question, it was a command. Annie felt herself melting beneath the smoldering desire that seemed to exude from his every pore. But she pulled back, reflexively.

"I love you, Annie," he said. "Whatever else you may think—or suspect—you must believe that."

Annie's mind reeled. It was what she had wanted to hear for so long! But how could she believe him? How could she trust this man who seemingly toyed with her emotions, who had never offered any explanation of his behavior?

She *wanted* to believe it, wanted it more than anything in the world. And now, with him tilting her mouth upwards, Annie found herself responding.

With a soft sigh of pleasure, she threw her arms around his neck, as if to take his kiss and draw it into her very soul. She swayed, wrapped up in his embrace, welcoming his gently probing tongue, his tender rediscovery. She felt herself consumed, caught up in the fiery bliss that recalled her most passionate memories . . .

Dear Reader:

After more than one year of publication, SECOND CHANCE AT LOVE has a lot to celebrate. Not only has it become firmly established as a major line of paperback romances, but response from our readers also continues to be warm and enthusiastic. Your letters keep pouring in—and we love receiving them. We're getting to know you—your likes and dislikes—and want to assure you that your contribution does make a difference.

As we work hard to offer you better and better SECOND CHANCE AT LOVE romances, we're especially gratified to hear that you, the reader, are rating us higher and higher. After all, our success depends on *you*. We're pleased that you enjoy our books and that you appreciate the extra effort our writers and staff put into them. Thanks for spreading the good word about SECOND CHANCE AT LOVE and for giving us your loyal support. Please keep your suggestions and comments coming!

With warm wishes,

Ellen Edwards

Ellen Edwards
SECOND CHANCE AT LOVE
The Berkley/Jove Publishing Group
200 Madison Avenue
New York, NY 10016

SULTRY NIGHTS
ARIEL TIERNEY

SECOND CHANCE AT LOVE
BOOK

Second Chance at Love books are published by
The Berkley/Jove Publishing Group
200 Madison Avenue, New York, NY 10016

To Susan and Bob
with love

SULTRY NIGHTS

CHAPTER

One

ANNIE CARROLL'S SLENDER high heels clicked precariously through the dark maze of cobblestoned streets. Nothing looked familiar. Pausing, she glanced down at the thick, cream-colored card in her hand. Hopeless, she thought, gazing around blankly. Where on earth was Royal Street? Even after four years in New Orleans, the French Quarter was still a puzzle to her.

As she tried to get her bearings, Annie felt a few light, moist drops land on her face. "Damn," she muttered softly, looking up at the clouds which nearly obscured the quarter moon. Just what she didn't need—rain! She was already running late, and she'd promised Nancy she would be there well before the gallery opened.

And now this. The hot bayou drizzle guaranteed to ruin the look of understated elegance that had taken her hours to achieve. Her usual on-camera work required a strictly tailored appearance, so Annie had used this occasion to get away from the professional restriction. The low-cut dress she wore was daringly backless. Its thin, sea-green silk clung to her slim, curving body like a second skin, and set off her fair complexion and wide-set hazel eyes to perfection. Her long chestnut hair, with its red-gold glints, was pulled up into a sophisticated knot, and tiny emerald earrings sparkled at her ears.

Now the dress was damp, and unruly wisps of hair were escaping around her face. Determined not to let the rain dampen her spirits, Annie looked around again and decided that Royal Street simply had to be the other way.

Wheeling about sharply, she hurried around a corner and stumbled into a large, masculine body. But before she could fall, Annie found herself steadied by the firm grasp of two strong hands on her waist. Startled, she looked up into a pair of amused, clear gray eyes. They slid up and down her body in a quick fluid appraisal, and seemed to enjoy what they saw.

"You really ought to be more careful on these rough streets." The man's voice was cultured, deep and soft, with just a hint of the New Orleans drawl in it.

"Excuse me," Annie replied, mustering her dignity. She was surprised to hear a slightly unsteady note in her voice. Tearing her gaze from the intelligent slate eyes and the finely structured, tanned face, Annie glanced down at the hands which lingered gently at her waist. His fingers, she noted, were long and sure—artist's hands.

Annie stepped back out of his grasp. Pushing a stray tendril from her brow, she offered the stranger her invitation. "Would you happen to have any idea how I get to this address from here?" she asked.

The man glanced at the invitation to the opening of Nancy's Gallerie Bleu while Annie covertly studied the unconventionally handsome face under its shock of thick black hair.

"You're all turned around." He smiled down at her, showing perfect white teeth. "Royal Street is around *that* corner, three blocks down." He pointed the way, his arm brushing her bare shoulder. "Would you like an escort?"

Annie took another step back. "No," she said hurriedly, "but thank you anyway." She felt the need to get away from this stranger. While he wasn't threatening, there was no mistaking the electrical charge she felt in his presence.

"Well," she smiled coolly, "good night."

"I think *au revoir* is more appropriate." He grinned lazily.

Annie shrugged and turned. As she walked away, she could feel his gray eyes burning into her.

The gallery was brightly lit. Stark white walls were hung with a stunning collection of black-and-white photographs, the works of three of New Orleans' most prominent still photographers. It had been a coup for Nancy to get these for the opening of her second gallery, and she'd made sure that everything—arrangement, lighting, the entire display effect—was perfect.

As Annie came breathlessly through the door, Nancy hurried up to her, her blue eyes concerned. "What happened to you?" she demanded. "People will be here in fifteen minutes, and I'm a nervous wreck."

Annie smiled reassuringly at her friend. "No need," she replied, gesturing at the walls. "This is stunning. Besides, where's Kevin?" she asked, looking around for Nancy's husband.

Nancy groaned. "He's still at the other gallery," she said. "Of all nights, this has to be the one that some dowager decides she wants to buy a painting."

"What's wrong with that?" Annie wanted to know.

"It's taking her *forever* to make up her mind which one of the landscapes she wants to match her daughter's room." Nancy shook her head. "What a way to choose art."

Annie shrugged. "It's paying your bills," she laughed. "Anyway, I'm here. . . . Anything I can do to help?"

"Oh, no . . . yes . . . I don't know." Nancy raked a hand through her light brown curls. "How about helping me pour some wine?"

"Sure." Annie set her tiny beaded evening bag in the back office and, moving quickly to the buffet table, grabbed a bottle of wine.

Within half an hour, the gallery was full. Wealthy patrons mingled with colorfully dressed artists, while serious art students exchanged comments with local critics. It was a terrific turnout for Nancy, Annie thought as she gazed fondly at her oldest friend, who was busily charming potential customers.

Ever since their high school days in St. Louis, Nancy's first love had been art. Studying design at Louisiana State University, she'd met and married Kevin, who shared her enthusiasm, and together they had created a harmonious life—a happy marriage and now, a second prospering gallery. What luck, Annie thought, grimacing at the memory of her own painful divorce. But that was all in the past.

"What are you making faces at?" Kevin's gentle voice interrupted her reverie.

"Oh, hi, Kev." Annie planted an affectionate kiss on his grizzled beard. "Was I making faces? Just thinking about . . . uh, things. Nothing important. Isn't this a great turnout?"

"Wonderful," Kevin agreed. He beamed jovially at the crowd. "What do you think of the exhibit?"

"Fantastic! But I've hardly had a chance to look," Annie confessed. "There's one photo over there that really caught my eye. I'll have to take a closer look when things thin out a little."

"Uh-oh, wine's about out." Kevin turned all business.

"Never mind, Kev, you go on and take care of the customers. I'll do the refills." Annie threaded her way through the packed room to the refrigerator in the office. Picking up a couple of bottles of chilled Chablis, she returned to the table and methodically filled a line of little plastic goblets.

"You're a lifesaver." Nancy grabbed the other bottle and helped Annie. "I can't believe how well this is going. Simply *everyone* is here."

Annie handed two filled glasses to a sedate gentleman and went back to pouring. "I like doing this. It's such a great opportunity for people watching. Did you see that..." The words died as Annie's attention riveted to a lithe figure strolling lazily through the gallery entrance. Heart pounding foolishly, Annie recognized the stranger who'd earlier given her directions. Did he have the nerve to follow her here?

"Annie! What on earth's the matter?"

Reacting to Nancy's shocked tone, Annie glanced down and saw that she'd managed to miss the last three goblets she'd been aiming for.

"I'm sorry, Nancy I...I just got distracted," Annie stammered in reply, inadvertantly looking at the tall figure in the doorway again.

Nancy followed the line of Annie's stare and laughed in sudden understanding. "Oh," she said, "now I get it. Well, relax, honey. You're certainly not the first woman Ellis Greystone has affected that way."

"Who? You mean you know him?"

"Not socially," Nancy replied. "But professionally, of course. He's a serious collector."

Annie's eyes narrowed. "And I'll just bet that art isn't the *only* thing he collects."

"Well, he's old New Orleans money, for one thing— and combined with those looks..." Nancy's voice trailed off meaningfully as Ellis spotted them, then made his way toward the table.

Yes, it was obvious, Annie thought, studying the man's casual but confident stride. This was someone who was used to getting what he wanted. She took a deep breath, composed her expression, and then looked up from under her long, lowered lashes to find him standing directly in front of her, grinning like a Cheshire cat.

"Well, hello," he said lazily. "You should have let me escort you here after all. Trying to break into the art dealing business?"

Annie automatically handed him a glass of wine, but before she could reply, Ellis shifted his attention.

"Kevin." Ellis smiled and offered his hand as Kevin moved up on Annie's left. "Where'd you manage to find such an adorable asset? She's a perfect decoration for this place."

"Annie?" Kevin replied, puzzled. "Why, she's not— *ouch!*"

Annie took her heel off Kevin's instep. Ellis Greystone was a snob, she thought angrily. He had looks and money all right, but his arrogance outweighed both qualities. Of all the nerve, talking about her like she was some sort of object, or as if she wasn't even in the room. Well, if that was Ellis Greystone's character, she didn't want anything to do with him.

Kevin gave her an odd look, but refrained from saying anything else, while Nancy tactfully steered the conversation to various pieces she thought might hold some special interest for Ellis. As Nancy guided him away from the table, Ellis glanced back over his shoulder and winked at Annie. Annie bit down hard on her bottom lip to stop herself from saying something that might ruin a prospective sale for Nancy. *A wink!* She was outraged.

Annie began pouring wine again, her hand now steady and determined. There was nothing like anger to restore equilibrium, she decided.

"What was *that* all about?" Kevin asked.

"What was what all about?" Annie stared innocently back at him.

"Okay." Kevin shrugged. "Have it your way, Annie. But it might be nice to have someone special in your life, you know."

"Kevin, I enjoy myself—and my life—just the way things are." Annie's tone was even.

"Oh, honey, you don't have to get defensive with me . . ."

Before he could finish the sentence, Annie sputtered, "And anyway, that . . . that . . . arrogant upper crust snob is your idea of someone special?"

"Well, you certainly seem to have caught his fancy. And, by the way, you do look terrific tonight."

"Thanks for the compliment Kev. But I'll pass on the rest of it. Ellis Greystone isn't my type."

Kevin laughed and shook his head. "All right," he said, amused, "we'll see."

Annie lifted her chin and narrowed her eyes. "You can handle the wine," she announced. "I'll see you in a bit."

Weaving her way through the tightly packed room, Annie found herself caught up in the excitement of the crowd, and drawn into the beauty of the display. The photographs were stunning—montages, character studies, nature scenes, surrealism. Annie paused occasionally to scrutinize a particular picture, and to say hello to the few people she knew. As usual, she thought admiringly, Nancy and Kevin had displayed impeccable judgment in their choice of work.

Annie's eyes were drawn again and again to a small, unobtrusive black-and-white photograph. The more she looked at it, the stronger its impact grew. A slender black tube of a vase containing one white rose stood against a rippling, satin-like background. Beside the vase lay a brilliantly sparkling glass slipper, turned on its side. One perfect white petal floated in the air midway between the rose and the slipper. Annie couldn't tear her eyes away from the consummate blend of illusion and reality, and she stood, entranced, no longer aware of the din around her.

"Lovely, isn't it?"

Annie turned, startled by the voice, and found herself face to face with Ellis. She looked up suspiciously to see if he was laughing at her, and was pleasantly surprised. His intense gray eyes were serious.

"Yes," she admitted cautiously. "I've never seen anything quite so . . ." her voice trailed off uncertainly.

"Romantic?" Ellis suggested, smiling down at her.

Annie shrugged. "I suppose. But it's more than that. It's almost, oh, otherworldly."

"I was watching you while you looked at it, and that's exactly how you looked—otherworldly."

"Oh." Annie felt herself start to blush. Someone from behind jostled her forward, and Ellis reached out to steady her.

"I always seem to be catching you when you fall . . . Annie, isn't it?" Ellis's hand lingered on her slender waist, his fingers brushing lightly over her bare back. "Why don't you and I go for a drink when the gallery closes?"

"No, thank you," Annie replied firmly.

"Come on, I think I can talk Nancy and Kevin into letting you go early." Ellis's tone was cajoling. "Besides, we could discuss art."

Annie's eyes widened in disbelief. Ellis just took it for granted that she would fall all over him when he mentioned "art" in that sophisticated, insinuating manner of his. Well, two could play this game.

She smiled up at him prettily and fluttered her eyelashes. "Really," she said softly, removing his hand from her waist, "I just can't."

"Why not?" He seemed amazed that anyone would turn him down. His sensual mouth widened into a grin. "Don't you think I'm capable of teaching you anything?"

Annie's hazel eyes turned frosty. "I sincerely doubt it," she snapped and walked away. Making a hasty retreat into the back room, she foraged through her purse and retrieved her gold compact. Staring intently into the mirror, she could see her cheeks had a flush that wasn't entirely due to blusher, and her eyes were throwing off emerald sparks—a sure sign of anger.

Calm down, she warned herself. None of this was worth getting upset over. At that moment, Nancy stuck her head around the corner.

"There you are," she said impatiently. "What's with you tonight, anyway? Of all nights, this is not the one to fall apart. I need all the support I can get, and here you are talking to yourself in the back room."

"Oh, Nancy, I'm sorry," Annie said contritely. "I'm fine, really. Is it wine time again?"

Nancy nodded, and the two of them took their places behind the buffet. While Nancy chattered busily about sales and patrons, Annie found herself scanning the room for a glimpse of Ellis. She spotted him, here and there, chatting with various guests, mostly attractive women.

With a mixture of resentment and reluctant admiration, Annie's eyes were drawn again and again to his tall, elegant figure, a combination of power and grace. His deep tan and his casual manner went with the playboy image Nancy had presented to her. He had probably never done an honest day's work in his life, Annie thought with disdain. Those looks went with sailing and scuba diving, with tennis and polo—not with work.

Still, she admitted grudgingly to herself, those eyes had both depth and intelligence. And she certainly hadn't spent so much time mentally appraising a man in years. In fact, since her divorce four years ago, dealing with romance had simply been something to be avoided.

A starry-eyed Annie married Gordon after her first year of college in her native St. Louis. The following year, when Gordon entered law school, Annie willingly dropped her own scholastic pursuits to help finance Gordon's expensive education. After all, selling advertising space for a local newspaper was not such a bad job, and, after three years, when Gordon got his degree, it would be his turn to put her through the rest of school.

But things hadn't turned out the way she planned. During the last year of Gordon's studies, she sensed a growing distance between them. Annie had tried to ignore it, chalking it up to Gordon's impossible schedule of full-time school and part-time law clerking at a prestigious St. Louis firm. When she managed to catch him long enough to question him, Gordon shrugged it off. Couldn't she understand the demands on him right now?

Two weeks after Gordon passed the bar and was formally accepted into the firm as a junior partner, he told Annie that he wanted a separation. They hadn't, he explained, grown together; they just weren't right for each other anymore. Too hurt to fight, Annie packed her things and left for New Orleans where she knew Nancy would give her comfort and advice.

Shortly after she arrived in New Orleans, Gordon had called her. He wanted a divorce—as quickly as possible. Suddenly, the pieces fell into place: Gordon was divorcing her to marry the daughter of the head of his law firm.

Hurt eventually gave way to fury, fury to disdain, and, finally, disdain to a clear-headed appraisal of her situation and her future. Bolstered by Nancy and Kevin, Annie enrolled at Tulane to finish her degree in communications and had not left New Orleans since.

Jolted out of her memories by a sudden flurry at the entrance to the gallery, Annie watched an exquisite blond woman literally sweep through the doorway, bubbling greetings right and left. She was accompanied by two remarkably handsome men who seemed to vie amiably for her attention. But the woman wasn't paying much attention to them. Instead, through the hugs and hellos that were being exchanged, Annie noticed that the blond appeared to be looking for something or someone in particular.

"Ellis, darlin', *there* you are," she trilled.

Well, well, Annie thought wryly. She'd found what she'd been searching for all right. Annie's eyes narrowed as she watched the woman greet Ellis with her lovely face turned up to meet his lips, and a graceful arm lingering possessively on his.

"Go on, ask." It was Nancy and she hadn't missed Annie's expression.

There was simply no way of keeping secrets from Nancy, Annie thought, shaking her head. "Okay, I'll bite. Who is she?"

"Don't you ever read the society page?" Nancy teased. "That's Camille Du Maurier. Her father is Senator John Jaynes. Very prominent family and all that stuff."

Annie's ears caught the different last names. "She's married?" she inquired hopefully.

"Uh-uh." Nancy shook her head. "At least, not at the moment. Though she has been a couple of times. Gorgeous, isn't she?"

As Camille Du Maurier, her hand still clinging to Ellis's arm, approached the table, Annie had to agree with Nancy. Up close, the Senator's daughter was a knockout. Silvery blond hair waved artfully around a sculpted face. Her large eyes were crystalline, an uncannily light electric blue; below the slender, turned-up nose, Camille's mouth was a sensual cherub's bow. Annie took in the sheer flowered chiffon dress, which simply wafted around the woman's body, the large flashing diamonds on her fingers and at her throat, and suddenly felt very young and very unsophisticated.

Camille, who obviously knew Nancy from other shows, greeted her cordially and praised her choice of artists, although her blue eyes traveled vaguely over Annie until Ellis spoke.

"Camille, honey, this is Nancy's new assistant, Annie—I'm sorry Annie, I don't think I caught your last name?" He stared mockingly at her.

"Carroll," Annie replied through clenched teeth.

"Charmed," Camille said airily, then did a slight double take, focusing sharply on Annie's face. "Don't I know you from somewhere?" she demanded. "You look familiar."

"No, I don't think so," Annie said sweetly. Didn't these people ever watch the news? And here she'd thought she was getting well known. Oh, well, she smiled to herself, another bubble burst.

"I doubt it, Camille," Ellis said smoothly. "Annie seems to be brand new here. As a matter of fact, I found her lost in the middle of the Quarter tonight."

Camille raised a cool eyebrow. "Oh?" she said, looking from Ellis to Annie and back again. "Is that why you didn't show up at my place to escort me?"

"Well," Ellis laughed, "I did get distracted. But then again, darling," he gestured expansively at Camille's two companions, "somehow I had the feeling that you wouldn't be left desolate and alone."

"Oh, Ellis," Camille pouted prettily, "you're impossible. Come on, I want to look around more." With a little wave, she dismissed Nancy and Annie and was gone, with Ellis in obedient tow.

"Why did you let him think you're my assistant?" Nancy's voice was puzzled.

"I can't stand people like that," Annie replied firmly. "He judges people by social status, not by who or what they really are."

"I think you're underestimating him," Nancy said. "But," she shrugged, "have it your way."

"Besides," Annie continued, a little defensively, "what difference does it make what he thinks? I'll never see him again anyway." She tossed her head in Camille's direction. "He looks like he's quite preoccupied."

"Oh, that." Nancy dismissed the idea with a wave. "Their families have known each other for literally centuries. They grew up together."

"Just old playmates," Annie said sarcastically. "Childhood sweethearts, right?"

"Actually," Nancy replied thoughtfully, "I believe they were engaged once—oh, years ago—but it never worked out. I don't know what happened, but Camille just keeps marrying other people."

"Well, it doesn't look like all the fire's died out to me," Annie retorted.

"Hmm..." Nancy regarded Annie with an amused glint in her eyes. "I do believe you just joined the living again."

"Honestly, Nancy." Annie shook her head impatiently. "First it was Kevin. Now don't you start in on me, too." Then she jumped, hearing Ellis's voice in her ear.

"Are you sure you won't change your mind?" he murmured. "Oysters, champagne, a walk in the moonlight? Or are you going to persist in abandoning me, leaving me to be just another one of Camille's pets?"

"Why don't you just try going home alone?" Annie replied sweetly, hazel eyes flashing as her heartbeat quickened. Ellis's physical presence made her nervous and snappy.

"I'm wounded," Ellis said mockingly. "You'll give me a bad reputation." Then his expression changed and he gazed down at her seriously. "Okay, Annie Carroll, you win round one. But you'll be seeing me."

"I doubt it." Annie turned her head away and busied herself cleaning up stray glasses. When she looked up again, he was gone.

Hours later, Annie found herself pacing restlessly around her apartment. Usually the high-beamed ceilings, graciously proportioned rooms, and her carefully selected furnishings provided a haven, a refuge from the outside world. But tonight, the normally soothing atmosphere seemed confining and she was unable to relieve her inner turmoil.

Carelessly kicking off her shoes and scattering her clothes, Annie grabbed a creamy satin robe from the walnut armoire. Pulling the wide sash tautly around her waist, she paused in front of her oak-framed full-length cheval glass. With her long tumbling chestnut hair and her face scrubbed clean, she appraised herself and saw a young-looking woman, pretty in an unpretentious way. Nice hair, yes; clear, sparkling eyes, yes; a slender, well-proportioned body, but...

Stop it, she told herself firmly, resolving to put Ellis Greystone, Camille, and the whole unsettling evening out of her mind. Work in the morning would demand her full attention and energy level. Discarding her robe, Annie climbed into bed and pulled the white feather comforter around her shoulders. A moment later, she threw it back. It was too hot to sleep that way.

Throwing open a window, she stared out at the moon. Finally, she sighed and returned to bed. Images of Ellis Greystone's piercing eyes and mocking grin appeared and reappeared as Annie tossed and turned, unable to get comfortable.

Annie remembered his hand on her waist and shivered pleasurably. After a while, she fell into a light, uneasy sleep, but it seemed that there was no escape: even in that shifting, suspended dream state, Ellis Greystone made his presence felt.

CHAPTER

Two

HURRYING THROUGH THE chrome and glass double doors that marked the entrance to TV news station, WJNO, Annie jogged across the newsroom floor. With only an occasional snap of an electric typewriter and the low-pitched thudding of the wire service teletype punctuating the morning lull, Annie stepped into her glass-walled cubicle and sank into her swivel chair.

Flipping the pages of her desk calendar, Annie saw that aside from the annual meeting with network lawyers, to discuss FCC language policy, there was nothing particularly pressing on her schedule for that day.

Fishing through her large leather shoulder bag, Annie found her much-used bottle of Murine and squeezed a shot into each eye.

"Morning, Annie. Ready for a cup?" A styrofoam cup of steaming black coffee suddenly appeared on the desk.

Annie looked up to meet the friendly eyes of Monica, the morning staff's communal secretary. "Thanks, hon," Annie said as she blew off the steam and took a sip.

"You ready?" Monica asked. Annie grimaced as the hot liquid slid down her throat, then nodded.

"A Mr. Jaglim, from the Mardi Gras Float Committee, called late yesterday saying he's got to cancel your interview. It seems he ran out of funds. Your cleaning won't be ready till Tuesday, and somebody named Guido says the car will be done this afternoon, soon as he gets the whatachamacallit from the warehouse. Otherwise, you've got nothing to worry about," Monica informed her as she dropped the message pad on Annie's desk.

"You'd think with Carnival coming up there'd be a little more excitement around here," Annie replied.

"Oh, don't worry, Annie, by the time this day's out, I'm sure you'll have a fine share of calamities, tragedies, and craziness to report."

"That's what I like about you, Monica, always something cheerful to say in the mornings," Annie countered jokingly.

"I aim to please," Monica replied, airily, as she turned and headed off to answer a nagging phone.

No sooner had Monica left the cubicle than the doorway was filled by the slim frame of David Sommers, WJNO's noted news director. "And how's my favorite on-the-spot reporter doing this fine mornin'?"

"Hi, David," Annie replied. "Just fabulous, as you can see."

Casually seating himself on the corner of her desk, the handsome executive broke into a smile. "Indeed I can," he remarked, his blue eyes beaming with the same warmth that initially intrigued Annie when she met David almost two years ago.

She was a senior communications major at Tulane the first time she saw him. Annie recalled that he was introduced as a guest speaker in one of the last seminars she had attended. David's tousled, sandy hair and blond mustache, combined with the light spring in his step, gave him a boyish, informal air. But as he addressed her class, it became obvious that David was a man of confidence. His manner before the 200 job-hungry seniors indicated that he'd done this several times before.

David didn't seem bored with the chore. In fact, he

offered sincere counsel, answering the students' questions with an understanding of the medium and an authority that showed Annie what professionalism was all about.

After the class broke up, Annie and a few other top seniors were invited to a luncheon at WJNO with David. In the noisy atmosphere of the studio commissary, she was pleasantly surprised to find herself completely at ease with the news director.

Gaining confidence by the minute, Annie was able to articulate some of her most creative ideas about broadcasting. Impressed by her enthusiasm, David fired off several questions. Although Annie didn't have all the answers, something about the thoughtful way she cocked her head and the spark in her eyes proved she was a camera natural and David felt she deserved a shot.

Annie was astonished when he hired her on the spot and she immediately questioned his motives. She need not have worried, however, because during the six months she was an errand girl for the veteran reporters, David never once made a pass at her. But he did watch her and her work closely.

As soon as she learned the ropes around the station, David promoted her to the lackluster position of Sunday backup reporter. And finally, after eighteen months, she'd earned her wings and David presented her with a plum—the six o'clock evening news. Throughout their working relationship David was always a pro and a gentleman. It was precisely what Annie wanted.

"How was the opening?" David asked and, for a moment, Annie, remembering her encounter with Ellis, hesitated.

"Uh, fine, actually," she replied finally. "A big turn-out, lots of browsers, and a good sampling of the upper crust."

"Nancy must've like that. She sell anything?"

"I'm not sure...probably, considering the well-heeled crowd." Annie realized she hadn't paid much attention to the opening after talking with Ellis and a wave of embarrassment suddenly washed over her. She made a quick mental note to call Nancy later.

"I wanted to make it myself," David continued, "but I didn't get out of here until about ten last night and with the rain and all," he shrugged apologetically. "Give my regrets to Nancy, won't you?"

"Sure, but don't you think you overdo it sometimes? Nobody else around here works as hard as you do, David. I swear to God, you'll be old and gray before you're forty," Annie teased.

"Perish the thought, child," David countered in mock vanity. "Besides, a little Grecian Formula will keep me looking spry for a long time and I've heard they do wonders with plastic surgery these days."

"Oh, David, you know what I mean. The extra duty just shouldn't fall on your shoulders all the time, that's all," she said sympathetically.

"Well, here's your chance to grab some of the glory, think you can find your way to New Orleans Memorial Hospital?"

"I think I can manage. What's up?"

"Seems Craig Bolding finally cracked up his race car and landed himself in the hospital."

"Is he hurt badly?" Annie's mind raced back to the dozens of films in which Bolding's handsome face had made millions of hearts flutter.

"Probably not," David continued. "but he is in surgery and the producers of his next film are very concerned. How about hopping out there and finding out the score?"

"Do I have a choice? Don't answer that. Got a crew?"

"Only the best for you, doll. You'll find Rudy and Joe out at the garage."

"Thanks, chief," Annie replied, gathering up her purse, a lined legal yellow pad, and an assortment of pencils.

Moving past David with an exaggerated salute, Annie crossed the now busy newsroom.

"Don't forget the meeting with the FCC boys at one," David yelled as Annie stepped outside, into the bright, clear New Orleans morning.

Approaching the WJNO remote van, Annie could see Rudy, the lanky Cajun soundman, joking with Joe, the balding, ruddy cameraman. As she watched the two easy-going technicians readying their stuff—Rudy threading up his tape recorder and Joe, attaching a freshly loaded magazine to his noiseless portable camera—Annie thought it must truly amaze her colleagues that these two seemingly lackadaisical guys could be such top-notch craftsmen. But, having worked with them on and off for the last two years, Annie knew she could rely on them for the best possible film coverage there was. An occasional card game and a few beers were their only vices, but these didn't make them any less effective on the job and Annie welcomed anything that made their work easier.

Picking up her step, Annie retied the floppy bow on her pearl gray, chiffon blouse. Pulling on the loose jacket to her mauve raw silk suit, she was suddenly grateful that even though her selection of clothing that morning was hasty, it nevertheless bore the mark of well-chosen elegance.

Just before Annie reached the van, Rudy looked up from his tangle of mike cables and broke into a toothy grin.

"Hey, Joseph, lookit here, we got one nice foxy lady comin' this way." Annie could see Joe swing out from the van's passenger seat and playing along, he produced a piercingly rich wolf whistle, then spouted, "Pinch me quick, Rudy, I must be dreaming."

"You guys..." Annie started. "Give me a break already."

In sloppy sync they replied, "Your wish is our command."

"C'mon, you jokers, we've got a date with a doctor."

Piling into the van, the trio headed out, waving past the studio guard in his kiosk, into the streets of greater New Orleans.

Settled into the van's cramped passenger seat, Annie pulled down the sun visor, gazed into the mirror clipped to the back, and went to work.

She checked her eye shadow first. Not enough, she decided and applied a thin layer of gray, enhancing her multicolored irises. A touch of mascara to her already thick curling lashes made her clear eyes appear even larger than usual. Just a touch of blusher and a quick outline of plum on her curving lips completed the process.

Satisfied, Annie began to jot down some pertinent questions for the upcoming interview.

From the back of the van, Rudy leaned his head between the two front seats and thrust five playing cards into Annie's hand. Joe, at the wheel, took another five from Rudy and a game of five card draw was underway. At a quarter a game, Annie could afford to indulge these two gambling fools for a few hands.

In between quarters and cards, Annie gazed at the colorful, old-world town, resplendent with beautiful gardens, quaint shops, and, of course, there was always the music.

Rolling down the window, she drank in the warm breeze wafting in from the mighty Mississippi. It was home, Annie thought. She couldn't imagine ever leaving it.

Joe swung the van into the hospital parking lot, pulling up to the entrance to the ancient brick building. Annie jumped out of the vehicle and immediately noted the presence of two similarly equipped vans. The logos of rival stations were visible on the doors and Annie could just imagine the media mob scene she'd have to fight through to get an interview with the hospital spokesman.

As Joe and Rudy quickly gathered up their bulky equipment, Annie grabbed an extra film magazine and the trio headed inside.

If the sleepy exterior of the building gave the place a tranquil, peaceful facade, inside was something quite the contrary. The polished floors echoed the rapid squeaking of nurses' shoes, hurrying to their duties. Dodging an orderly propelling a gurney, Annie and the crew approached the information desk.

"Can you tell me where the press conference on Craig Bolding will be?" Annie asked the college-aged woman working the desk.

"Follow the green line and turn left at the third elevator. You can't miss it."

"Thank you," Annie said moving off with her crew in tow.

As they traipsed down the neon-lit, spotless corridors, Annie could see several people carrying cameras, lights, and recorders, pushing through a doorway up ahead.

Approaching what evidently was the hospital conference room, Annie saw the friendly face of rival newscaster, Tom Rowley, sporting a beautiful, pancake makeup tan and every hair in place.

"Anne Carroll, my favorite colleague. My, but you're looking lovely this morning."

"Thanks, Tom, you're looking swell yourself," Annie replied in a bored voice. This wasn't the first time she had indulged Rowley as he fished for a compliment.

Annie couldn't imagine a more vain personality than this slick reporter, but he was also good at his job and Annie knew she couldn't afford to take the competition lightly.

Bumping and jostling, Tom and Annie moved into the tightly packed room, alive now with the hubbub of an eager press awaiting the hospital's statement.

"Hey! That's my foot!" Annie looked up to see Rudy apologizing to another station's cameraman. Meanwhile, Joe slyly moved in the man's place, grinning at Annie as he took a advantageous position in front of the un-occupied speaker's podium.

Annie turned back to Rowley. "Any word yet on Bolding's condition?"

"I don't know, babe, but I found out from the sweetest little blond nurse, that they brought in some hotshot surgeon from the university. Nothing but the best for America's heartthrob, I suppose," Tom offered with a sigh.

A dark-suited bureaucrat stepped up to the podium and tapped on a goose-necked microphone. Assured it was on, he cleared his throat and requested the group's attention, although it was his without asking. The news teams quickly huddled around him, lights glaring.

"First of all, I'd like to say that Mr. Bolding has come out of surgery and all signs point to a full recovery," the man stated and immediately the various reporters fired off a score of questions.

"Please, I can't answer you all at once," the flustered spokesman yelled over the cacaphony. Turning his head this way and that, he spotted a tall figure entering the room. "If you'll kindly settle down for just a second, you can give your questions to the man who performed the surgery on Mr. Bolding."

Straining on tiptoes, Annie peered over the several heads in front of her to see a man approaching the speaker's podium. He appeared tall and graceful as he moved closer. His operating room greens were rumpled and showed traces of sweat, giving evidence that he'd just come from surgery.

As the doctor reached the microphones, he took off his green head covering and Annie suddenly froze. It couldn't be! But there was no mistaking the shock of black hair, those clear, sharp gray eyes, that deeply tanned handsome face. A slow chill crept up Annie's spine as she stared, dumbfounded, at Ellis!

"Ladies and gentlemen, I'd like to present Dr. Ellis Greystone, renowned heart specialist and chief of surgery at Tulane University Medical School. Dr. Greystone was kind enough to rush over here and supervise the operation on Mr. Bolding. So if you all care to settle down a bit, I'm sure he'll try to answer your questions."

All at once the reporters started up again and Annie, still stunned, was lost in the shuffle as the others jostled around her, eager to catch Ellis's attention.

"Hold on now, one at a time, one at a time. I'm sure we'll get to everyone." Ellis's manner was cool, easy, yet authoritative.

Expertly handling the unruly group, Ellis fielded their questions, saying that while yes, Craig Bolding was still in guarded condition, the prognosis was good and he would definitely recover fully. It seemed that the actor was unable to avoid a multi-car collision in a formula race in Baton Rouge. Three broken ribs weren't usually cause for concern, Ellis continued, but one of them poked through a lung and another was dangerously close to his heart. It was a rather simple operation, but the hospital staff, and Bolding's anxious producers, didn't want to take any chances, so they sent for Ellis.

Annie felt like a fool. It wasn't often she misjudged someone so badly. She had been sure that Ellis was an arrogant playboy, with nothing to offer a woman beyond an occasional fling and a continual condescending attitude. Yet here he was in the flesh. He had handled a life-threatening situation with total control and now he dealt with the press with equal ease.

The initial attraction she'd felt at the gallery, which seemed so easy to dispel with her preconception of the man, now returned with renewed intensity. Everything about him was electrifying.

Annie was jolted out of her deep thoughts by a nudge in the ribs. "Annie, c'mon, wake up kid." Rudy's concerned face reminded her that there was work to do.

Quickly gathering her wits, Annie shoved her way up front, stood next to Joe and asked in a loud, surprisingly firm tone, "Has Lena Forest been notified and if so, has she had a chance to see her husband?"

Ellis turned his attention to Annie and, after a momentary start of recognition, he broke into a subdued grin.

"As a matter of fact, immediately after he came out of the anesthesia, the first thing he asked for was Lena." Suppressing a smile, Ellis continued, "She was busy rehearsing for a Broadway play in New York and a commercial flight wasn't available. But a charter pilot I know was most agreeable, and the several cases of champagne that Craig offered didn't hurt either. She arrived about twenty minutes ago and, I'm sure you'll understand, there won't be any other visitors allowed to see him for the rest of the day."

The conference lasted another ten minutes, and even though Annie was able to come up with several intelligent questions, most of her attention remained focused on that lithe, masculine presence before the microphone.

Glancing at his watch, Ellis signaled that the questioning was over and walked out of the room.

The reporters and crews filed out and Annie, more composed now, slowly followed Joe and Rudy as they headed for the parking lot.

"Excuse me, Miss Carroll?" Annie turned to see Ellis walking up to her, still in his greens.

"Yes, *Doctor* Greystone?" Annie replied, curtly.

As Ellis caught up to her, Annie readied her defenses, but somehow there was an allure about this man that overwhelmed everything. How close could she get before it was too late to turn back? Annie's heart began to beat faster.

"Last night at the gallery, I thought you looked familiar," Ellis began, apologetically. "I guess I should be more up on who's who in this town. Anyway, I'm sorry I misjudged you. Can you forgive me?" he said disarmingly.

Annie flushed as she recalled his earlier assumption that she was simply a gallery decoration. But Ellis's bright smile, accentuating the mild cleft in his chin and the single dimple at the edge of that sensuous mouth easily melted all hostility.

"I suppose so. No harm done," she replied, trying not to sound nervous. Tearing her eyes from his mesmerizing gaze, Annie started to turn away. "If you'll excuse me, I've got a crew waiting to get this story back to the station."

Ellis followed her out of the building and, reaching possessively for her arm, steered Annie under a wide, shady poplar tree.

She stared at his strong, sure hand and felt a shock flood through her whole body. Her eyes traced a line up Ellis's own arm, across his muscular chest, past the wisp of black hair showing through the open V of his shirt, up and across his strong jawline and finally rested on that curving mouth.

Ellis began in a strong, sure voice. "What I mean to say, Annie, is that it's not often a man gets a chance to meet a woman with a sharp mind to go along with such a pretty face. Won't you allow me the opportunity to make up for my mistake?"

A tentative "yes" was forming on Annie's lips when Ellis continued, "I'd like the opportunity to explore your charming assets more fully."

With this cocky suggestion, it seemed to Annie that his sensual smile had become a leer. So she'd advanced from gallery decoration to pushover, had she? Annie's anger flared up like a sleeping cat doused with a pail of water.

"And does that mean I'm supposed to jump right into your bed, *Doctor?*" Annie spat back, shaking her arm loose.

"Hold on, now, don't get..." but before Ellis could plead his case, Annie fired again.

"You're so smug, Ellis Greystone, you think any woman would jump at the chance to be in your arms. I can just imagine you in your ivory tower hospital, fawned over by all those adoring nurses and candy stripers. Well, if you think I'm falling for your tired old line, you're in for a surprise!" Annie fumed.

She turned on her heel, but once again Ellis grabbed her, this time by both shoulders, forcing her to look at him.

"Dammit, Annie, do you think I fall for just any woman who comes along? I think you're something special. All I *want* is a chance to prove it."

Ellis's fevered intensity surprised Annie and, for a moment, she felt he would force his lips on hers. But Ellis loosened his grip, allowing Annie to regain her composure.

"Don't waste your time," Annie snapped. "I don't

like snobs and you don't really want a woman who won't be molded to your every desire."

To Annie's surprise, Ellis replied thoughtfully, "Perhaps you're right. Maybe I am a snob. Sometimes I get so caught up in my own affairs I forget how other people feel. If you haven't already guessed, I'm dedicated to my career, Annie, and sometimes I push everything else aside. But I also know there's more to life than just work and so do you." Ellis's voice warmed huskily with the declaration. "Let me take you out tonight, Annie. Let me show you what kind of magic this old town has to offer." Again he leaned close to her and Annie felt mixed emotions coursing through her. Ellis was too powerful a force and she didn't want to be swept away.

"No," she managed, turning her head, breaking his grip, and moving away.

"I'll call you, Annie, and I'll keep calling until you come around." Ellis's final words contained an irritating confidence.

Flouncing off, Annie raised her chin. "Don't bother. Save your dimes," she replied, equally confident as she jumped into the passenger seat of the van and slammed the door behind her. Turning to her crew, Annie still seethed. "Let's get this crate on the road."

Reacting in mock fear, Joe threw the van into drive, peeled a bit of rubber, and then eased the heavy vehicle out of the parking lot.

Annie snuck a quick glance into the side-view mirror and saw Ellis emerge from the shade of the poplar tree and stand in the sun, watching her drive away.

Rudy poked his head between the seats again, dealt three hands of "21" and waited for Annie's bet. "Annie?" he queried, noting her intense stare out the window.

"Deal me out," she snapped and Rudy exchanged a puzzled glance with Joe.

The camerman quipped, "Looks like what the doctor ordered didn't sit well." Annie turned a withering look on him.

Rudy touched a finger to his tongue, then placed it against Annie's hand. He mouthed a loud "hiss" and turned to Joe. "This is one hot momma we got here, Joe."

Annie tried to glare at him, but the Cajun's knowing wink broke her mood and all three burst out laughing.

At ease again, Annie dropped a quarter on the van's center console and said, "Deal me in."

With the air cleared and the hot breeze blowing through her hair, Annie thought about her neatly ordered life.

With Rudy, Joe, and David, she had a rare and wonderful working relationship and above all, she had fought hard and earned their respect and her independence. At this moment, keeping her independence seemed harder than ever before. But there was one thing she was sure of: no one would ever *take* it from her.

CHAPTER

Three

BACK INSIDE THE station, the pace had quickened perceptibly. More people were in evidence, and the sound of humming electric typewriters was pronounced. As Rudy and Joe headed for the editing room to run the tape, Annie waved them off.

"Got a meeting in a few minutes," she called, checking her watch. "I'll catch up with you later and take a look, okay?"

It was a familiar routine to all three of them, and Joe just smiled. "Whatever you say, boss lady," he replied, disappearing down the well-lit hall.

"How'd it go?" David swung around the corner, passing the crew, and followed Annie into her cubicle.

"No problem," Annie replied airily. "Bolding's going to be fine. The whole thing was really just a glamour puff piece."

"Well, well," David teased. "Aren't we getting picky about our stories? Not everything has to be a major political event or a catastrophe to rate a spot on the six o'clock WJNO broadcast, you know."

"Annie," Monica stuck her head into the office, "someone named Ellis Greystone called twice. He said to tell you that it's important. Here's his number. He wants you to call him back as soon as possible." She

31

handed the pink message slip to David to pass to Annie.

Annie raised one eyebrow. "Call him back?" she said coolly. "Fat chance. Just toss that in the basket, would you, David?"

But David was staring down at the slip, his expression bemused. He looked up at Annie calculatingly, then grinned. "Ellis, huh?"

Annie's hazel eyes narrowed. "What do you mean, 'Ellis huh?'" she asked suspiciously. "Don't tell me you know him, too?"

"Oh, you might say that." David's blue eyes held a mischievous twinkle. "We only played basketball together in high school and roomed together in undergraduate school before Ellis went off to medical school and I became an illustrious news director."

Annie sank back in her swivel crair with a groan. "I don't believe it," she muttered. "This town is getting smaller by the minute."

"How did you hook up with Ellis, anyway?" David asked curiously.

"We didn't *hook up,* David. I, uh, we just met each other last night at the gallery opening. Then today, well, he was the supervising surgeon on the Bolding operation. No big deal." Annie shuffled some papers around on her desk, avoiding David's penetrating gaze.

"Hmm." The news director tamped down the sweet-smelling tobacco in his pipe, then lit it thoughtfully. "And he's called twice already? Not bad, kiddo. Usually it's women falling all over Ellis, not vice versa." He chuckled quietly.

"I'm sure anyone with an ego that size can get over a little rejection," Annie stated firmly.

"Ellis's ego, as you call it, is really only involved in his work—and rightfully so," David protested.

"What do you mean?" Annie asked reluctantly.

"He's brilliant," David said matter of factly. "His research into heart disease and deterioration is the most innovative and far reaching in the entire field. He's had offers from every major research center in this country, some with unlimited funding behind them, too."

"Then why is he still in New Orleans?" Annie's curiousity was piqued now.

David shrugged. "This town. You know it's got its own special magic. I guess we'll lose him one of these days, but he'll put it off for as long as possible."

Annie wondered fleetingly if beautiful Camille Du Maurier might have something to do with Ellis's decision to remain in New Orleans. But that was one question she wasn't about to ask.

"Well," she said brightly, changing the subject, "we should be getting to our meeting, don't you think?"

David nodded his agreement, and stood courteously aside so Annie could precede him through the door. As they hurried across the newsroom floor and turned the corner into the hall leading to the conference room, Joe's head popped out of one of the editing rooms.

"Lookin' good, sugar," he called, giving Annie the thumbs-up sign. "You photographed even better than usual today."

"Yeah." Rudy's voice floated out unseen from somewhere behind Joe. "Too bad we didn't get some footage of you and the Doc. Whoo-ee—temperatures *risin'!*" His laughter was loud and appreciative.

"Rudy," Annie protested, "would you just cool it, please? I'll be in after the meeting to check it out, and then I've got to write the copy for my intro. No more smart remarks, okay?"

"Yeah, boss," Joe and Rudy chorused, still laughing as they slammed the door.

Annie looked up embarrassed to find David staring

speculatively down at her, and she felt a warm flush rising from her throat.

"Sparks flying?" he suggested mildly.

"No!" Annie snapped. "No sparks, no interest, and no more questions."

"Yes, ma'am." David bowed with mock courtliness. "Whatever you say. But you know, Annie, the newsroom is an absolute hotbed of information. You can't keep any secrets around here."

"I'm quite well aware of that, David," Annie replied grimly. Oh, was she ever aware of it, she thought. It was hard enough to get to—and maintain—a top-level reporting spot as a woman, without any nasty gossip attached to it. But, with David's guidance and friendship, she'd managed it. She'd seen and heard enough in the past two years to be certain that if she looked cross-eyed at someone at ten in the morning, by ten fifteen, it would be all over the floor—with questions and speculation flying. Annie was determined not to lose her hard-earned reputation as friendly, straightforward, and strictly non-flirtatious—particularly over one ridiculous incident. Damn Ellis Greystone, she fumed, then took a deep breath to settle her feelings down, as David opened the door to the conference room.

The meeting stretched out over a good portion of the afternoon and Annie found herself growing restless. What they were discussing was important: language policy tended to be a recurring, frequently argued issue. It seemed the list of what reporters could and could not say over the air changed from day to day. Nevertheless, Annie's mind wandered to the morning's footage and she felt an irresistible curiosity about how it looked. Finally, the conference over, she headed down the hall toward the editing room, flagging Joe on her way.

He was right. The footage *was* good and her questions

had come across with an extra bit of spirit and spark. Too bad it hadn't been a hotter issue, she thought regretfully.

But Joe's reaction was just the opposite. "This is terrific, kid," he said admiringly. "Bolding's such a hot number, this has to go national . . . and I bet New York chooses to use your coverage as the pickup."

Annie's eyes widened in delight; she'd forgotten about Bolding's celebrity status. "Do you really think it looks that good?"

"Po-so-tively!"

"Okay, what've we got here?" David crowded into the room and shut the door behind him. He watched as Joe reran the tape. "Fine." He confirmed the option. "Get it ready for New York."

"David!" Annie shrieked, giving him a brief hug. "My first national, Oh, I'm so excited! Thank you!"

"Don't thank me." David smiled down at her. "It was only a matter of time. Now, Miss Carroll, where's your intro copy?"

"I'm on my way." Annie dashed from the room and sprinted for her cubicle. What a coup, she thought, settling herself at the typewriter and banging out a snappy thirty-second lead in to the hospital coverage.

"Are you done?" Monica peered in. "I need that for the monitors, on the double."

"One minute," Annie promised, quickly rechecking what she'd written. "Okay, here you go." She handed the typed copy to Monica, then sank back in her chair, smiling. Seven o'clock national news was the best exposure a newscaster could hope for and it was hers on a fluke. What a wonderful day, she thought.

"Fifteen minutes, Annie," Monica's voice interrupted her reverie. "Get yourself down to makeup."

Freshly lipsticked and powdered, every hair combed

neatly into place by the fussy hairdresser, Annie walked out onto the set and took her place beside Jackson Cahill, WJNO's anchorman. Cahill was in his late forties, and had graying hair and finely etched lines around his intelligent eyes. An aloof, but thoroughly professional newsman, he generally kept his distance from the other newscasters.

Tonight, however, he smiled broadly at Annie. "I saw your footage, and heard about the pick-up," he said. "Congratulations, Anne."

"Thanks, Jackson," Annie replied warmly. A compliment from Cahill was a compliment indeed.

"Sound check," someone yelled.

"One-two-three, reporting live from Saturn," Annie said into her mike.

"Okay. Thirty seconds—everybody quiet!"

Jackson remained precisely as he was, Annie composed a calm, intelligent smile on her face, and the news began.

After the broadcast was over, people gathered around the monitors to watch the national news. Annie's footage was shown close to the end, and when it ended, she found herself breathing a sigh of relief as she gathered up her things.

"Annie, hang on a minute—you can't go home now!" It was David, sandy hair touseled, a broad smile on his face.

Annie promptly put her things down. "Why?" She gazed eagerly up at him. "Is something hot breaking?"

"No, sweetie," David laughed. "What I meant was, this is an occasion, and I think we should go somewhere and have a drink to celebrate."

Annie hesitated only a moment, then got into the spirit. "Sure, that sounds great," she decided, realizing she was too keyed up to go home right now anyway.

"Oh, listen, I just remembered—can you give me a lift home, afterwards? I never got over to the shop to pick up the car today."

"No problem," David replied smoothly.

"Okay. Let me get my office straightened up and check what's on the calendar for tomorrow then," she paused and put her hand dramatically to her forehead, "take me away from all this. I want to be alone."

David threw back his head and laughed appreciatively. "Calm down, Sarah Bernhardt."

"That wasn't Sarah Bernhardt," Annie replied indignantly. "It was Greta Garbo."

"It's a good thing you limit your acting ability to the news camera," David winked. "See you in a bit."

Half an hour later, Annie and David strolled casually into Diablo's, an informal waterfront club featuring some of New Orleans' best jazz. Tonight, there was an upbeat, melodic quartet with a wonderful, sultry sax. The club was dark and intimate, and David secured a river view table for them.

Annie sank into the soft leather chair and stared out at the wide Mississippi, lapping gently at the shore, and gleaming silver in the moonlight. Its beauty never failed to touch her, and she sighed at the sight of the river and the sound of the wailing sax.

"Are we going to toast to your success, or are you just going to sit there gazing wistfully out the window?" David teased gently.

"Oh!" Annie picked up the large snifter in front of her and swirled the Courvoisier around, watching the thick, amber liquid slide heavily on the sparkling crystal. "Let's toast, by all means."

David raised his glass, his blue eyes warm with affection. "To both of us, then," he began. "To your present success—may there be much more in the future. And to me, for being able to pick the best."

Their glasses clinked, and Annie took a sip, her eyes dreamy with the hopes of a bright future.

"Annie, can I ask you something?" David said solemnly.

Puzzled by the request, Annie just nodded. David had never asked permission before.

"What are you doing with your life—I mean, outside of your career?" David looked concerned. "You don't go out much, do you?"

Annie was startled and caught off guard. In all the time they'd worked together, David had never shown the slightest interest in her personal life.

"What do you mean, David?" She stared quizzically at him. "If you're asking if I'm involved with someone and successfully keeping it a secret from WJNO's vigilant staff, the answer is no."

David shook his head. "Of course not, that's not what I meant. I guess I'm just curious. After all, we've known each other for quite a while now, and you still seem so exclusively involved with work. Oh, never mind, honey, I didn't mean to pry."

Annie stared down at her drink, thinking about David's remarks. David, her friend, her mentor . . . if he wanted an explanation, it was the least she owed him.

"No, David, it's okay, really. It's not prying. It's just that my divorce was really painful . . . at the time," she clarified. "And since then, my life has turned around so drastically . . . I've grown so much. I'm, well, so much happier now. I guess I just don't think about that part of my life much any more."

"Annie, I know you've grown. Don't forget, I've seen a good part of that happening. But I'd hate to see you cut yourself off from that other important part of living because your marriage wasn't a happy one..." David smiled ruefully. "My marriage wasn't exactly a major blockbuster of a success either, honey, but I'm still looking for the right lady."

"Are you, David?" Annie asked, surprised. David was a perfect gentleman, closed-mouthed about his ex-wife, Liz, though that didn't stop newsroom scuttlebutt about Liz's latest boyfriend, Liz's latest public antics, Liz's latest spending spree. Flamboyant, wild, unstable Liz— the last person on earth that anyone would have picked for David Sommers. But David *had* picked her, and it had been a perfect disaster. Over the past two years, Annie had seen David with any number of pretty women at various social functions, but it had always appeared casual. To hear David confess that he was actively searching for a new, serious romance came as a total shock.

"Of course, Annie. I want a *full* life, not just half. How about you?" David's eyes were warm, searching hers for a clue.

"I haven't given it much thought," Annie confessed slowly. "And I really don't know if that's been sort of accidentally-on-purpose or if it really hasn't mattered to me. I just know that up until now, all my plans for the future have been centered around my work... and nothing else."

"Is this conversation as intimate as it appears, or can I join you two?"

The low, drawling voice was unmistakable. Annie took a long, deliberate sip of liquor before she raised her eyes to meet Ellis's piercing slate stare.

"Why, Ellis! Hey, ol' buddy, sit right down." David gestured at the extra chair.

Annie felt the flush rise from her chest to her forehead. She'd been set up!

"Right, ol' *buddy*," she echoed David sarcastically, then threw a scorching look at the wide-eyed news director. She turned to Ellis, and continued with sugary sweetness, "But why bother to ask how intimate the conversation is? Didn't you guys have all that planned out in advance, too?"

"Annie," David protested, reaching for her hand.

"Stop it, David." Annie jerked her hand out of his reach angrily. "Isn't it enough that your little maneuver worked. What more satisfaction do your collective egos need?" She grabbed her purse and started to rise, but was pulled back into her chair by Ellis's firm grip on her wrist.

"Enough," he said quietly. His eyes, she observed, were serious; his mouth set in a firm, straight line. "It's my fault...not David's," Ellis continued as Annie sat rigidly. "I talked him into bringing you here. But we certainly didn't plan the conversation or anything else." He met her unforgiving green stare and added impatiently, "God, Annie, if I waited for you to call me back, I'd be waiting forever. And I don't have forever."

"Take your hand off my wrist," Annie said coldly.

"Why don't you stop being so defensive?" Ellis demanded.

"I hate games," Annie replied evenly. "I'm not very good at them. And this seems very much like a game to me." She threw a nasty glance at David. "Just like the good old days when you two used to play basketball together, right?"

"Calm down, Annie." David's tone was sober, but his mouth was starting to curve upward. "After all, it isn't every day that I get to play Cupid for hotshots like the two of you."

Annie bit back a reluctant smile, then, catching David's blue-eyed twinkle, began to laugh. Why not?

she thought giddily. Everything else today had been topsy-turvy and unpredictable. It made perfect sense that her day would end with the omnipresent Ellis Greystone sitting beside her at a jazz club.

Both men visibly relaxed as Annie laughed.

"Truce?" David enquired.

"Well..." Annie said reluctantly, "all right, for the time being. But I owe you one," she warned.

David rolled his eyes. "And believe me," he told Ellis, who was quietly observing them, "she means it." He glanced at his watch. "Well, looks like it's about time for me to wander on home—" The unspoken question hung in the air.

"Annie?" Ellis's voice was low and persuasive. "Won't you stay for a bit and have a drink with me? Please?"

Why fight such an elaborate—and flattering—setup, Annie thought, meeting the challenge in his slate eyes.

"I'd like that, Ellis." It was the first time she had called him by his name, she realized, feeling a slight tremor, as if some small, intimate barrier had just been broken.

David breathed a sigh of relief and rose from the table gracefully. "Don't forget, you're on six and eleven tomorrow, Carroll."

"Yes, boss," Annie snapped, then added sweetly, "Isn't it time for you two to give each other the secret ol' buddy handshake now?" She fluttered her eyes at David, who burst out laughing.

"Good luck, Ellis. She's always like this." He waved, and was gone.

"Are you?" Ellis asked softly, gazing intently into her wide, sparkling eyes.

"Am I what?"

"Always like this...flippant, defensive, whatever

you want to call it?" Ellis's gray eyes were probing, and, just as she had been at the hospital, Annie was once again overwhelmed by this man's sheer physical magnetism.

She caught her breath. "Don't you think that's kind of insulting?" she queried. "You're making assumptions, and you really don't know anything about me, or what I'm like." She tore her eyes from his and stared down at her glass.

Ellis reached out and gently caressed her throat, then lifted her chin, forcing Annie to meet his gaze again. She was acutely aware that her pulse had leaped, and wondered nervously if he could feel its throb where his fingers rested lightly on her soft skin.

"That's precisely why I'm here," he said. "I want to know everything about you—who you are, what you are, where you came from and where you're going, what you love and what you hate—*everything.*"

Annie laughed shakily. "That's a pretty tall order for one night, don't you think?" She tried to keep her tone light, and, turning her head slightly from his touch, lifted the brandy snifter to her lips. Ellis's hand moved, feather light, across her cheek, then dropped to the table.

"I told you a few minutes ago, I don't have time to waste."

"What's the rush?" Annie sipped her brandy. Ellis might not have time to waste, she thought, but all this was happening too fast for her.

He broke into a sudden, engaging grin, and Annie found herself smiling back. "Well," he admitted, "I guess I'm just the impatient type. Actually, I'm leaving for Johns Hopkins in the morning, and I won't be back until the midnight shuttle flight tomorrow night. I just couldn't see waiting over twenty-four hours before I saw you again."

Annie laughed, amazed. "Impatient?" she echoed. "There's got to be a stronger word for it than that!" It was, she realized, quite a compliment. Somehow the boldness of this self-assured, handsome man wasn't grating on her nerves the way it had the night before. He obviously knew now that she was no toy, that she was his equal, and his interest in her seemed frank and genuine. Annie felt herself relax a little, and gazed at him with an open look. "Where would you like to begin?" she asked.

Ellis motioned the waiter to bring them two more Courvoisiers. "Date, place, and time of birth," he replied promptly. "Childhood diseases, education . . ."

"Wait a minute." Annie raised a protesting hand. "This sounds like a medical questionnaire, *Doctor*. You're off work now, remember?" Laughter floated out of her.

Ellis shook his head in rueful acknowledgment. "You're absolutely right," he replied. "Okay, let's start over. What about work? How did you get into newscasting, and what do you want to do with it in the future?"

The melodic jazz strains wove in and out of the conversation like seductive magic, and Annie found herself revealing her background and aspirations. He, in turn, spoke of medicine and its overriding importance in his life. He'd always known, he confided, that he'd be a doctor; he hadn't known just how far it would take him or how it would dominate his existence.

"That's why I'm flying to Baltimore tomorrow for a preliminary conference," he explained. "I'm being considered for Head of Surgery at Johns Hopkins."

"Oh." Annie felt a sudden pang of disappointment. "So you'd consider moving away from New Orleans?"

"I don't really want to." Ellis shook his head. "Everything I care about is here," he added, gazing deep into

Annie's eyes. "But the research facilities I need to continue my work just aren't available in this city. And I can feel that I'm getting close to a major breakthrough, something which could save thousands of lives." He reached for Annie's hand, turning it over. "Anyway, I'm not going to have to make the decision tomorrow." His slender fingers played lightly over her palm. "I think, Ms. Carroll, that we've been serious enough for one evening, don't you? Let's go for a walk. There's something I want to show you."

"All right," Annie agreed, her curiosity piqued. She stretched as she stood up, and was aware that Ellis's eyes never left her.

Outside the smoky club, the air was warm and humid. Even with her jacket off, Annie could feel the heat of the night closing in on her like a cloak. As she and Ellis strolled down to one of the innumerable docks near the club, only the click of Annie's heels broke the thick silence.

"Here we are." Ellis gestured at the sleek white boat moored to the dock beside them.

"She's beautiful," Annie gasped, taking in the lines of the fifty-foot cabin cruiser. Gleaming, powerful in the silvery moonlight, the craft barely swayed with the lapping of the big river beneath her.

"She is beautiful," Ellis agreed proudly. "Her name's the *Aurora,* and she's all mine. Want to come aboard?"

Annie felt a moment's hesitation. What was this really an invitation to? But Ellis was already aboard, leaping on with catlike agility, holding out a strong, beckoning hand to her. Taking his hand she climbed onto the deck. A bit off balance, Ellis steadied her lightly, his hands on her waist.

"Back to where we started?" he murmured quizzically, his face close to hers.

Annie felt the pounding of her heart. "Not quite," she replied softly. She could feel his breath against her hair, feel the tension which emanated in waves from his lean, strong body.

"Good," he whispered huskily. "That's exactly what I wanted to hear." He brushed her neck softly with his lips, barely grazing her warm skin, and Annie shuddered, almost dizzy from his touch.

Sensing her confusion, Ellis drew back for a moment and dropped one hand, leaving the other poised lightly at her waist. "Come on, Annie," he said gently, "let me show you around."

Not trusting her voice, Annie simply nodded her head and let Ellis lead her. With her slender hand clasped firmly in his, they strolled around the immense deck, admiring the polished brass and teak railing, pausing to take in a breathtaking view of the Mississippi as it rippled south toward the gulf. Below deck, Ellis delightedly showed off the trim, sparkling galley and two large, comfortably furnished staterooms.

In the elegant main salon, Annie dropped his hand with an exclamation. It was perfect: glass and teak book-cases were nestled on either side of a formal dining set. Overstuffed, green velvet couches and a polished copper Dutch fireplace enhanced the gracious, yet homey room. Ellis observed her with a smile on his sensual mouth as she walked around, examining the beautiful objects and nautical paintings.

Annie could feel the gentle slap of the tide against the boat's hull as she opened a porthole to look at the moon. Faint jazz sounds from Diablo's drifted into the room as she gazed, entranced, out over the river.

"Annie." Ellis's voice was commanding, throaty.

She turned, startled, to find him right beside her, his slate eyes delving into her soul. "Oh, Annie," he repeated softly, one arm going swiftly around her waist, the other hand tilting her head to meet his kiss. His mouth descended on hers, incredibly gentle, she thought fleetingly. Then, all thoughts were swept away as the kiss grew in intensity. Ellis's tongue explored her mouth demandingly, probing deeply, educating itself to her needs and desires; and Annie found herself responding hungrily, her lips exploring his with equal intensity, her hands on his wide shoulders.

"I haven't been able to think of anything but you since this morning," he murmured, leading Annie to the couch and pulling her down with him. His eyes were fevered, blazing with his hunger for her. "Tell me you feel the same," he demanded, one finger tracing the outline of her curving mouth.

"I . . . I don't know," Annie whispered, mixed emotions and desires coursing through her body.

"Yes, you do," he insisted, folding his arms around her.

She felt the strength in that lean, hard body as he pressed her against him, kissing her lips, her neck, running his hands possessively along her slender waist and hips. His tongue was demanding now, and Annie gasped and tried to pull back as he made short work of the buttons on her sheer blouse.

"No, Ellis," she protested weakly, melting under his expert touch. His fingers skimmed lightly over the silk chemise, teasing and exciting; Annie felt her nipples harden, straining against the delicate fabric.

"Don't say no," Ellis whispered against her throat, his mouth moved tantalizingly down her body. As he pulled gently at the silk, kissing her breasts, Annie felt a fire sweep through her.

It's too soon, she thought, too soon for this. Any further and she would lose all control. With this realization, she tore herself away from his touch.

"What's wrong?" he asked cupping her face gently between his hands.

Annie didn't meet his gaze immediately. She busied herself redoing her blouse, then, at last, looked up. "I can't, Ellis. This is all too fast for me. I just don't live like you."

"What do you mean by that?" His gray eyes looked genuinely puzzled.

Annie knew that for her, love and desire were inextricably entwined: one couldn't be any good without the other. But how could she say that to him without sounding like a little fool?

She breathed deeply and looked squarely into Ellis's eyes. "I'm not into casual affairs," she stated quietly.

"Oh, Annie darling." His slate eyes held a mixture of desire, laughter, and some other, unidentifiable emotion. "Neither am I!" He threw back his head and laughed. "Neither am I." Suddenly his expression turned serious. "But I make up my mind very quickly. When I see something I want, I go after it." He kissed her lightly. "Now, will you stay with me, or do you want me to take you home?"

Annie's hazel eyes widened in surprise and admiration. He really wasn't going to try force or persuasion; she was free to choose. She reached out a hand and stroked his angular cheek gently. "Take me home, please."

The drive back was very quiet. Only Ellis's midnight-blue Jaguar purred softly through the now-deserted streets. As Ellis pulled up in front of her apartment, Annie gestured for him to stay in the car. She needed to be alone to think.

"It's okay." She spoke softly, her hand on the door latch.

Ellis drew her to him briefly. "I was serious, Annie, about knowing what I want." His lips lingered on hers for a moment. "But it has to be mutual." His eyes searched hers questioningly.

"I need time," Annie replied.

"Take all the time you want," Ellis replied. Then, as Annie stepped out of the car, he grinned. "But I'll be calling you the minute I get back."

Annie stared at him for a moment, confused by the emotions and desires this man had so easily awakened in her. It had been a long, long time since anyone had affected her this way, and the complications it could bring to her life were unknown and could be unwelcome. Quelling the arousal in her mind and body, she told herself there was nothing left to say, not here, not now, at any rate.

"Good night, Ellis," she said softly, shutting the door behind her. At the wrought iron gate leading to the courtyard of her building, she turned suddenly and looked back, just as the sleek, powerful car disappeared silently around the corner.

CHAPTER

Four

ANNIE SHOVED THE shift lever into first and zipped her pearl-white Alfa into the heavy traffic. Moving in frustrating stops and starts through the crowded streets, she headed for the French Quarter. Guido's wizardry with machines was apparent as the finely tuned engine purred, despite Annie's somewhat heavy-footed driving technique. The nimble little roadster responded beautifully, even though an irate cabbie didn't appreciate it one bit when Annie cut him off to make a right turn.

But Annie's thoughts were only half on her driving, as if she was on auto pilot, her preselected destination looming in the distance. Up ahead, she could see Nancy's Gallery Bleu; hopefully Nancy would be there.

Annie prided herself on her usual composure, but since Ellis's sudden appearance in her life, she was frazzled and confused. The hard years spent building up her self-confidence, the layer upon layer of callous she'd formed over the wound left from her broken marriage, all seemed stripped away, leaving her emotionally vulnerable.

He was just a man, she told herself sternly. Sure he was handsome, but she dealt with handsome men every day in her line of work. Sure, he was a successful surgeon, intelligent, powerful, and alluring. Normally, even this wouldn't have profoundly affected her. But what kind of man could stare into her eyes and make her spine tingle, make her heart flutter, make her very being pulsate with desire? Was it love? Or was it Annie's old naïveté getting the best of her?

Slipping the Alfa into a rare, curbside parking spot, Annie spotted Nancy through the gallery's front window and sighed gratefully. She simply had to talk this out.

The tiny brass bell on the French door entry tinkled as Annie moved inside. Nancy perked up from the clutter of papers on her desk. "Hi, Annie. Be with you in a second," Nancy greeted, shoving a pencil behind an ear, continuing to gather together the mess in front of her.

"No rush, I just dropped by to see if you had time for a cup of mud," Annie replied, barely able to hide the anxiety in her voice.

"Sounds like a great idea. I'll be ready in a minute . . . I swear, I never knew there could be so much paper work in this business. Seems like every day somebody's buying or selling something. . . . I guess I shouldn't complain, though. Royal Street is really the place to be."

"It's good to see *somebody's* doing well," Annie let slip.

Nancy caught Annie's tone and raised her brow. "Let me file these away and grab my purse," she offered.

As Nancy grabbed a stack of brimming folders, Annie strolled around the gallery showroom, half-heartedly gazing at the various works. She stopped at a small blank spot on one of the walls, disappointed not to find the one photograph she really cared about.

"Say Nancy, where's that little black-and-white photograph you had hanging here?"

"Which one, hon?" Nancy asked as she emerged from the back room, slinging her purse over her shoulder while grabbing up a ring of keys.

"The one with the vase and the slipper."

"Hmmm, I was at the other showroom, yesterday.... I guess Kevin must've sold it," Nancy shrugged.

"Oh..." Annie's voice trailed off as she looked away.

"C'mon, I need a break," Nancy said, firmly, as she lead Annie to the door.

Annie appreciated the quiet, charming little pâtisserie Nancy choose in the Vieux Carre. From their window, they could look out across the old square, at the buildings with their elaborate, beautifully detailed iron railings. It was amazing how few things had changed from a bygone era in this anachronistic city.

A white-coated, black waiter set two steaming cups of dark coffee and a small tray of croissants in front of them and, with a polite nod of his head, moved to another table.

Nancy picked up one of the cups and, raising it, offered, "Here's to success, yours and mine." As Annie picked up her cup, the two women clinked them together and took a sip.

After savoring the rich, spicy "Louisiana Mud," Annie collected her thoughts and plunged right in. "Nancy, I need some advice," she said.

Nancy picked up one of the delicate little French rolls and replied, "I could tell you didn't drop by to discuss the latest in mid-length skirts, Annie, so shoot." She bit into the croissant and waited patiently.

"Well... it's difficult to explain, but since I met this man my whole world seems to be turning upside down."

"This man?" Nancy teased, gently. "You mean Ellis Greystone, don't you?"

"Yes, I mean Ellis Greystone." She shook her head ruefully. "I just can't get him off my mind. He seems to care about me but I just don't know. He's got everything most women could want, but it's all happening so fast . . . too fast," she said wearily.

"So?" Nancy replied. "Count your blessings, child."

"I'm a grown woman, Nancy, and I should be in control of all my faculties, but this man . . . I don't know if he's telling the truth half the time or just trying to add a notch to his list of conquests. Damn! He would have to be good looking," Annie said as she knit her brow in frustration.

Nancy brushed the crumbs off her chin and quipped mildly, "What are you afraid of, Annie? I bet inside he's like all men—just a pussycat, that is if you know how to handle them."

"That's easy for you to say," Annie replied. "You've been lucky with Kevin. I can see the trust you two have in each other."

"I guess I *have* been lucky," Nancy agreed, "but believe me, Annie, I still know what you're feeling." Placing her hand over Annie's, Nancy continued, "Hon, I think your meeting Ellis could turn out to be something truly wonderful, especially if he's as interested in you as he seems to be. C'mon, how long has it been since you've been serious about a man, four years, now?"

"Well . . . I guess it's been a while, but that's got nothing to do with it." Annie faltered with the sudden realization that indeed, it had been a long time since she'd been so seriously affected.

"It's got everything to do with it," Nancy insisted. "You're afraid to fall in love, Annie Carroll, afraid you'll get hurt again. But you can't simply run away from someone because of what he *might* do to you. Believe me, if you go into everything looking for the negative, you'll only be hurting *yourself* in the long run."

"Nancy, I'm trying to put things in their proper perspective. I'm trying to be open-minded about Ellis, but I'm not so sure I'm ready to be involved in a relationship again. I'm on a roll at work. Things are finally going my way and an uncertain romance could really throw a monkey wrench into all my plans," Annie stated, her voice shaky.

Nancy swirled a spoon in her coffee. "You don't expect me to buy that, do you? What plans could be so one sided that there's no room for love—unless you're thinking of becoming a hermit. You're too young to be a serious candidate for spinsterhood," Nancy teased. Then, pointing her spoon like a lance, she continued: "Just because Gordon turned out to be such a louse doesn't mean Ellis will. I know your divorce was painful. It can be a real shock to discover that someone you trusted, someone you sacrificed for, was really a rotten apple. But honey, you can't let one bad experience stand in the way of the rest of your life." Nancy jabbed her spoon in the air to emphasize what she wanted to say. "Let's face up, Annie, you're not the naïve little girl from St. Louis anymore. Give yourself some credit. It takes a strong, independent woman to build her life and career the way you have. If your heart and passions are awakened by a man, well, then you must be aware of something within him that's worthwhile. Trust your feelings a little bit—you've got good judgment."

"More coffee ladies?" the white-coated waiter asked as he stepped up to the table.

Nancy drained the last drop from her cup and held it out for the man to fill. "Thank you. This is delicious."

Annie nodded her head and held her cup out for a second round of the potent beverage. The waiter obliged and Annie stared after him until she was certain he was out of earshot. "Tell me about Camille Du Maurier."

Nancy stopped in mid-sip, peering at Annie over the lip of her cup. "You've got nothing to worry about there," she said firmly.

"I'm not so sure. She's used to getting what she

wants," Annie surmised, "and from what I've seen, she wouldn't mind having Ellis firmly secured in her stable."

"So what else is new? Camille's got a big stable, but I don't think Ellis is the kind of man who likes to stand in line," she said meaningfully.

Annie turned her head to the window and stared at the old square.

"Here, eat this other croissant," Nancy gently coaxed as she held the pastry aloft in Annie's direction.

"Nancy!" Annie turned her head back to her friend, a note of impatience in her voice.

"Okay, okay, but there's really not much to tell," Nancy finally offered. "Their families go back years, maybe even a couple of centuries. According to Kevin— my information is second hand by the way—Ellis and Camille were playmates as kids. They grew up together. They did the usual stuff—picnics, hayrides, cotillions— all very civilized, of course. You know how those rich folks are. Camille was quite a tomboy it seems, until she came back from some fancy finishing school up North. The little girl came back a grown woman with a new set of goals. Evidently she had her sights set on Ellis." He probably never had a chance, Annie thought to herself.

"When he was an undergraduate at Tulane, Camille made a big show of watching Ellis play on the basketball team. You can believe me when I say her painted toes and soft-bottomed feet *never* stepped into a pair of sneakers. She was decked out to the nines all the time." Annie could just imagine how "decked out" Camille could be as she remembered the woman's entrance the night of the gallery opening. "Anyway, when Ellis graduated and decided on medical school, Camille was fit to be tied. She thought he'd be right for politics and she was sure her daddy could help the boy out. After all, who could deny Ellis and Camille were made for each other, and that someday, Senator Jaynes would have a fine, up-standing son-in-law? Leastwise, that's what Camille wanted everyone to believe. Camille pushed Ellis until an engagement between the two was announced and the wedding date was set with all the lavish details well covered in the local society pages. Then, suddenly, the engagement was off."

Annie's interest was piqued. "Off . . . just like that? What happened?"

Nancy sighed and shrugged her shoulders. "The best Kevin could come up with was that Ellis wanted more than to have his future handed to him on a plate, tailor made. He had a talk with the Senator and evidently the old man was impressed with Ellis's determination because he encouraged Ellis to pursue his medical career and Camille, if she could, would just have to wait."

"I can't imagine that one waiting for anything." Annie replied, grabbing the last half of croissant before Nancy could sink her teeth into it.

"Well, believe it or not, she did. For two years anyway, although everyone swears she was seeing men on the sly, while publicly pining away for Ellis. I guess time finally took its toll because Camille couldn't wait any longer. She got married, got divorced, got married again, et cetera, et cetera."

Annie wasn't satisfied. "From the way she handled Ellis at the opening, I'd say she's still set on him."

"C'mon, Annie. You've seen how that woman operates. She's spent a lot of years working those fluttering eyelashes and that charm routine down to a fine art. She's that way with just about any man. Ellis sees right through it, believe me."

"I suppose so, but he's still up on her current affairs. He did say she asked him to escort her to your gallery," Annie said defensively.

"Oh, they've stayed friends all these years. They're more like brother and sister now, there's nothing crazy about that. He didn't escort her though, did he?" Nancy's question seemed to clear the fog of uncertainty in Annie's mind. As the two women looked affectionately at each other, Annie couldn't help but smile.

"Will there be anything else, ladies?" Annie and Nancy looked up at the waiter who once again stood at the table.

"That's all, thank you," Nancy answered and she quickly snatched the check from the small plate he placed on the table.

"Give me that, Nancy," Annie protested. "After all, I'm the one who asked you out."

"No way. Besides, I ate all the croissants." Nancy dismissed the matter with a wave of her hand.

While Nancy fumbled through her purse for some cash, Annie once again turned to the window and squinted as the afternoon sun glinted off the shops and buildings, sending warm beams through the little panes of the restaurant window.

At least Nancy had been frank, Annie thought to herself. Perhaps she could afford to let her guard down a bit.

"Merci beaucoup, madame." Annie turned to see the waiter beam his thanks for Nancy's generous tip. But before the man walked off, he seemed to notice something about Annie and turned to her directly, "Excuse me for staring, *madame,* but aren't you Anne Carroll?"

"Why, yes..." Annie answered tentatively.

"We watch your newscast," the waiter volunteered. "In fact, my little girl, Louise, won't let us watch any other news. She'll be so excited when I tell her I waited on you. Could I trouble you for an autograph, perhaps on this napkin?" He pulled a clean, linen cloth from the next table.

Annie couldn't contain the blush that spread across her cheeks. "Sure I'd be happy to . . . Louise is it?" Annie took the pen that he offered as Nancy looked on with an amused grin.

"Yes, you know, she's quite taken with you," the man continued as she wrote. "She talks about going to college, maybe being a newscaster like you are, Miss Carroll. Louise says you're the best reporter on the air."

There had been few opportunities for celebrity status during her budding career and normally, Annie could care less if people spotted her as a television personality. Her main interest was journalism. But the waiter's innocent request, and the fact that his daughter chose to emulate her, was a real boost for her ego.

Handing back the signed napkin, Annie thought of something. "How old is Louise?"

"She'll be fifteen in September, Miss Carroll."

"Well, if she's serious about getting into journalism, have her give me a call and I'll give her a tour of the news facilities at WJNO. She can see for herself what the job is like," Annie offered.

"Merci, madame, merci," he gushed and instead of shaking the hand that Annie held out to him, he bent low from the waist and elegantly kissed her on the fingers. With another smile, he was off.

Driving back to Nancy's, Annie couldn't suppress the grin that kept tugging at the corners of her mouth. She knew she would have to deal with the conflicts that were running through her head, but for the moment, the waiter's simple praise warmed her like sunshine peeking through the clouds after a spring shower.

Annie pulled up to the gallery and Nancy found the car door handle. Before she got out, Nancy turned to Annie and put a hand on her friend's shoulder. "Look, honey, I don't want you to back down from anything, and you shouldn't sell yourself short. It's not easy to trust anybody. But you should be willing to give Ellis the benefit of the doubt. After all, not everyone gets a second chance at love." Nancy leaned over, gave Annie a hug and a kiss, then stepped to the curb.

"Thanks, Nancy," and with a wave and a shift into first gear, Annie slipped off into traffic.

Annie made it through the six o'clock report, giving a perfunctory performance, unable to muster enthusiasm for the rather ho-hum news of the day. Even though she had settled down from her earlier anxiety, the long day simply got longer. She watched the score of technicians move about the stage, trailing cables, repositioning lights, chatting with one another, as they prepared for the next newscast later that night.

Annie strolled up along the narrow, dangerous cat-walks, high in the rafters of the sound stage, watching the people below her move like industrious ants. It was a good place to think.

By the time of the eleven o'clock recap, Annie worked by rote, bemusedly turning from one camera to the next, following the little red signal lamps on the top of each one as they focused on her. One blinked on, then the other and Annie reacted like a spectator at a tennis match as the director, in his glass-walled control booth, signaled his camermen and punched up the camera he wanted to cover her.

Annie knew, of course, that even though she tried to read her copy with aplomb, she was coming over rather flatly. Her director told her as much and Annie felt a sudden pang of remorse. She hoped that if Louise was still up watching the news, she wasn't disappointing the girl.

When the show was finally over, Annie unclipped the little microphone from her blouse and heaved a sigh of relief.

"You can say that again," her fellow anchorman, Jackson Cahill said wearily, as he stepped off his naugahide stool and walked off the set, following Annie.

Strolling out of the cavernous soundstage, Annie and Jackson exchanged the usual shop talk, but her heart wasn't in it. They reached his dressing room and Jackson suggested Annie get a good night's sleep. He promised that if there wasn't any decently exciting news tomorrow, he'd go out and make some himself.

After removing most of her makeup, Annie checked back into her cubicle. She could see that David was still in his office, burning the midnight oil. The thought of knocking on his door crossed her mind but it was getting late and if David was still hanging around here, he must be trying to finish up something important. There was no point in interrupting him and making the amiable executive stay around even longer.

"Annie?" She looked up to see James, the late-shift gofer, peer into her office. "You get the package I left?"

"Hello, Jimmy. What package?" She asked.

"I set it on the chair. There it is." He entered the little room, crossed over to the chair by the door and retrieved a flat rectangle, covered in brown wrapping paper. Annie examined the innocuous looking package, not knowing what it was or who it was from.

"Thanks, Jimmy. Say, you're here a bit late, aren't you?" She turned her attention from the package to the bleary-eyed college freshman.

"You can say that again," he agreed, checking one of the many wall clocks, which indicated the time in various parts of the world. "I've still got to study for a final on advertising marketing, so see you tomorrow."

Annie made one last effort to clear her desk. Just before she got up to leave, she turned her attention to the package. A pair of desk scissors made short work of the wrapping. A small note tumbled out and Annie opened it. A wave of surprise swelled over her, followed by a flood of warmth.

"Please let me give you this, Annie," it read, "I saw the way you looked at it and knew it was love at first sight. . . . Ellis."

Annie folded back the tissue paper covering the inner contents of the package and revealed the little black-and-white photograph she had seen at Nancy's gallery opening. It was beautiful yet unpretentious in its small, modest frame. Ellis could have bought her anything, but somehow he'd known that nothing could be so dear, could mean so much as this simple, elegant gesture.

Annie walked to her car, with the precious object tucked tightly under her arm. As she headed home, her mind raced, wondering what Ellis could have been thinking when he bought the photo for her. How could he know how much it would mean to her? Could any man be that astute concerning such a simple little thing?

As she neared home, Annie could almost see Ellis's charming smile and suddenly, she heard the echo of his voice, "On the midnight flight home . . ."

Annie screeched to a halt, hesitating only for a second before she swung her car in a brisk U-turn in the middle of the road, then powered off in the opposite direction. With her heart beating wildly, Annie urged the little car onward, heading straight for the airport.

CHAPTER

Five

THE DRIVE TO the airport was mercifully short and with the attendant problems of wondering which airline Ellis had taken, and finding a place to park, Annie didn't have much time to reflect on her actions. She pulled the little Alfa into a passenger loading zone and hopped out of the car. Pausing to get her bearings, Annie then headed resolutely for the dual Atlantic and Delta terminals. More than likely, one of these airlines would have a midnight shuttle flight.

It turned out to be Delta and, as Annie walked up to the young man seated at the information counter, she felt slightly embarrassed to ask if Ellis's name was on the passenger list. Nevertheless, she made the inquiry and, when the young man told her that he wasn't allowed to reveal that information, Annie managed to flash her best smile at him.

Reaching into her purse, she produced her press credentials. "Couldn't you bend the rules, just this once?" she cajoled sweetly. "It's official."

He looked like he was barely out of college and he melted before Annie's lovely smile and the sudden recognition that she was a local celebrity.

"Oh, Miss Carroll!" he exclaimed. "I didn't recognize you at first. Is this for WJNO?"

"Yes, it's for an exclusive I'm working on," she assured him conspiritorially, as he reached for the passenger list."

"Dr. Greystone *is* on the flight," he informed her, "and they should be landing in, uh, about four minutes. Gate seventeen," he added helpfully, pointing the way.

"Oh, thank you *so* much." Annie favored him with another perfect smile, then turned and walked rapidly in the direction he'd pointed.

"Hope you get the scoop," he called out as she walked away. Annie felt a little guilty. But she quickly rationalized that it was rare that she resorted to this sort of deception—certainly not as often as some of her colleagues. Besides, she smiled to herself, this *was* an exclusive of a sort!

Standing in the white glare of the terminal lights, Annie began to lose her nerve amidst a wave of second thoughts. What was she doing here at this time of night, meeting a man she barely knew? What did she want? Even more important, just what did she expect would happen as a result of her impulsive gesture? This was so unlike anything she'd done before. How out of character for Anne Carroll, Miss Cautious, to forget propriety, to show up at midnight to meet a plane which was carrying the one man who might, with a casual sweep of a hand, break down all her carefully built defenses.

Annie pivoted uncertainly, debating whether or not to make a dash for her car when a metallic voice announced over the public address speakers that Flight 402, from New York, Baltimore, and Atlanta, was now debarking at gate 17.

Taking a deep breath and running a shaky hand over her unruly knot of hair, she turned to face the rush of incoming passengers.

Ellis was one of the last to come straggling off the

plane. There was no mistaking that shock of midnight-black hair and his purposeful stride. Annie felt her heart leap at the sight of his sharp-hewn, handsome features. He looked tired and preoccupied, his thick brows furrowed in some private thought and Annie wondered about the results of the conference at Johns Hopkins. Then, as he drew near where she was rooted to the floor, Ellis lifted his gaze.

It might have been coincidence, Annie thought, but without hesitation, Ellis focused directly on her. Was the physical magnetism really that strong? Annie had no time to puzzle it out because Ellis strode directly over to her, stopping a scant few inches from her upturned face.

"Annie . . ." Ellis's voice was soft and warm as he leveled his slate eyes, searching deeply into her own wide hazel ones.

"I . . . I wanted to thank you for the picture," Annie stammered, feeling like a complete fool. She silently chided herself for this impulsive meeting and felt her cheeks flush as an amused smile played across Ellis's lips.

"You drove out to the airport at midnight to thank me for a present?" he echoed sardonically. His slate gaze swept over her in a nearly physical caress and Annie's eyes fell before his penetrating stare.

Damn this man, she fumed to herself. She'd never met anyone who had the power to dissolve her poise and reserve with so little effort. Well, she'd offer to drive him home and that would be that. But the words died in her throat.

Ellis grasped her arm with a strong, practiced hand, and pulled her close to him. There was no teasing in his voice when he continued, "Forgive my reaction, Annie, I hadn't expected such a pleasant surprise." Before she could reply, Ellis's mouth descended on hers in a light, lingering kiss. Holding her slender body against his taut, muscled torso, Ellis murmured against her mouth, "Miss Carroll, you're full of delightful surprises."

Annie was amazed by her immediate response to his embrace and she swayed against him, feeling his thighs and chest pressing heatedly against her. For a dizzy moment, she gave in to the feeling, then reminded herself where they were.

"Ellis, stop," she gasped, drawing back slightly, but still holding him firmly.

"Okay," he grinned obligingly. "Let's go get my luggage and then we'll go home." There was no doubt in his voice. They were going home, to his home, together. And then . . . Annie shook the haze away.

"All right," she said tremulously, as they moved along the long tunnel that led to the baggage area. Ellis retrieved a leather bag from a circular conveyor belt and, flinging it easily over his shoulder, said, "Where's your car?" Annie silently guided them out to the little Alfa.

"Want me to drive?" Ellis asked.

Annie eyed him suspiciously. "I'm fine, thank you," she replied a bit sharply. "Perfectly capable of driving my own car." As if to prove her words, she threw the car into gear and screeched out of the loading zone. "Where are we going?" She added as an afterthought. She glanced over at Ellis who had finally removed the silly grin from his face. He gave her directions to his Saint Charles Street residence then settled down into the leather bucket seat and relaxed.

Warm, moist delta wind whipped around Annie's face as she drove. She glanced covertly at the long, muscular legs of her companion as he sprawled comfortably, and she felt a shiver creep up her spine. There was no denying the sensual spell that this man cast over her and yet, what if that was all it was, she wondered. If only she could be sure it was more . . .

"What is it, Annie?" Ellis's husky drawl broke in on her private thoughts. She cast a brief glance at him; just long enough to see the sharp, appraising gleam in his steely eyes. She had the uncomfortable feeling that he could read her thoughts.

"Nothing," she replied, shakily.

"Nothing?" Ellis repeated. "The usually reserved, articulate Anne Carroll shows up at midnight at the airport—very unexpectedly, I might add. And that selfsame young woman says practically nothing and is anything *but* articulate when she does manage to stammer out a few words." His strong fingers traced a lazy path down her neck, flooding her with warm tremors.

Annie glared at him but was surprised to find a look of compassion in his eyes. He wasn't teasing. Could it be possible that he really understood the turmoil he'd thrown her into?

"We're here," Ellis announced, and Annie pulled the Alfa into a circular cobblestone driveway in front of an elegant mansion. She stared at the weathered gray stone exterior, the wrought-iron balconies, the wonderful amalgam of Louisiana style.

"This is beautiful, Ellis," she murmured, managing to get the sentence out without stumbling over her words.

"Come see the inside," he urged, his eyes dancing. Annie shrugged. Why not? She'd come this far already and she could always make an excuse and go home, if she chose.

Inside, the gracious old house reflected the masculine, tasteful dictates of its owner. Ellis guided her through the cathedral ceilinged foyer into a large, comfortable library. Wood paneling gleamed handsomely on the walls and comfortable deep chairs and a sofa, done in charcoal and burgundy, were randomly placed.

There were floor-to-ceiling bookcases, filled with leather-bound volumes, lining two walls. Muted gilt lettering reflected off the subtle, low lighting. Two other walls featured what Annie realized must be part of Ellis's private art collection. As she gazed around, his deep voice broke into her thoughts.

"Why don't you pour us some brandy," Ellis suggested, pointing to the bar in one corner, "while I go change into something more comfortable."

He disappeared and Annie wandered over to the bar, where she located the brandy and two crystal snifters. She paused thoughtfully, then poured the amber liquid. Ellis seemed to be taking her appearance at the airport in stride, she mused. Which was more than she could say for herself. She chided herself for the hesitant, juvenile way she must have sounded to him and took a silent vow not to let it happen again. After all, she reasoned, Ellis seemed acutely aware of her mixed emotions. He certainly wasn't going to force her into anything she didn't want to do. If only, she sighed, she knew exactly what that was.

Leaving the glasses on the polished mahogany bar, she wandered over to a wall full of track-lit pictures, and examined them. Ellis did display impeccable taste, she thought. This wall held a combination of dreamy, impressionistic paintings. Among them she recognized a Pissaro and a tiny Degas, plus bold, modern canvases, including a Rothko and two by Pollock. She shook her head, amazed at his ability to purchase whatever his taste decreed.

"Is something wrong? Why are you shaking your head?" Ellis's amused voice took her by surprise and Annie turned, startled to find him lounging against the bar, the two snifters in his hands.

"I was just wondering what it would be like to be able to buy one of these." Annie gestured at the paintings. "Although I'm not sure that it's really right to own such beauty."

Ellis's eyes lit up as he replied to her comment. "I don't really think of it as owning beauty," he replied softly. "After all, these will be passed on . . . to children if I have any, or to museums some day."

Ellis moved beside her and handed Annie one of the glasses, clinking it lightly with his. She was once again aware of his overwhelming masculine presence. He'd changed into faded jeans and a lightly ribbed, white V-neck pullover sweater. It was the most informal attire Annie had ever seen him wear and the casual clothes fit him perfectly. The worn jeans molded his lean, muscled thighs, the pullover revealed a tanned chest with curling black hairs, and set off his broad shoulders to perfection.

"Do you approve?" Ellis remarked as once again, he seemed to walk right into her thoughts.

Annie felt an unexpected streak of mischief and boldness and, with her wide hazel eyes alight, her full mouth tilted upward, she stared directly at him. "I approve," she breathed.

"Good," he replied in his husky voice. His piercing eyes appeared ready to devour her and Annie momentarily felt self-conscious, seeing her tousled hair and flushed face reflected in his eyes. Ellis reached for her glass and removed it from her hand, setting both glasses down on the bar. Then his hands were on her waist. "Annie darling, look at me," he commanded.

Annie raised her eyes obediently. She felt a loss of breath as she met Ellis's smoldering stare and became conscious of the light pressure of his sure, strong fingers.

Ellis stared down at her silently for a long moment, drinking in the glow which seemed to radiate from within her. Then his mouth began a tantalizing, slow descent onto hers. His lips caressed her soft full mouth, tasting, exploring, biting softly at her full lower lip. Annie felt, rather than heard, the small moan at the back of her throat as her lips parted under Ellis's soft assault. She welcomed the invasion of his tongue as it explored the soft lining of her mouth, probing, coaxing such an intense response from her that it seemed they would drink each other up. She felt Ellis's strong supple fingers under her blouse, tracing tantalizing patterns on her sensitive skin, drawing her closer to the warm length of his body.

Annie's slender body swayed willingly against Ellis. Caught helplessly in her own passions, she felt herself arch against the length of him, seeking the heat and hardness of his body, demanding the power of his embrace. His unremitting, driving masculine desire found a perfect match in her primitive feminine need.

Annie gasped as Ellis pulled away from her, only to find herself being pulled down onto his lap as he sank into a deep velvet loveseat. One arm cradled her shoulders while the other stroked the base of her throat. Her pulse was leaping as Ellis stared at her, his eyes smoky and soft. He kissed her again and Annie's arms went obligingly around his neck. As the kiss deepened, Ellis shifted his eager lips and sent them burning down the slender column of her throat. She felt her hands twisting through his black hair, found herself trying to pull him even closer . . . deeper.

His hand slid possessively lower, unbuttoning her blouse, exposing the soft curves of her breasts, covered only by her lacy wisp of a bra. As one hand curled around her shoulder, holding her a willing captive, the other pushed gently at the lace, tugging it aside, so he could draw light, shivering circles around her nipples. Annie's breath came in gasps and she arched herself against his palm, wanting his touch to go on and on. His sure, sensual stroke made her writhe in his lap, leaving no uncertainty about his own rising response to her. Somehow, her silk shirt was gone, her bra was off and Annie lay in his lap, naked to the waist, completely revealed, totally under the spell of his expert caresses.

"Annie." Ellis voice filtered through the haze that surrounded her and Annie looked into his stormy, smoldering eyes.

"What?" she replied in a voice she didn't recognize. Why had he stopped? Her body cried out for fulfillment, yet Ellis was holding back.

"Annie darling, tell me that you want me," he demanded. "Tell me you want me as much as I want you." His gaze was both passionate and serious and Annie knew the decision was completely hers. Despite his passionate arousal, Ellis would stop what they had started if she didn't give herself willingly and knowingly to him. And she also knew that, if indeed she did give herself to him, there would be no turning back. Her surrender would have to be complete; there would be no more defenses in their way—only the passion of their lovemaking and whatever inextricable results came from this most intimate entanglement with this complex, intense man. And just as surely as she knew this, Annie knew that she could not, would not turn away. No matter what the consequences, she was here and she would be his.

She reached up and gently stroked his cheek, feeling the little nerve ends in her fingers respond to his bristles. "Yes, Ellis," she said softly. "Oh, yes. I want you." She pulled his head down to hers and found his mouth with her own, sealing the promise of her words. The clip fell from her hair and Annie felt the long, silken auburn strands tumble down around their faces. Ellis, stroking the soft tangled mass, groaned softly.

Holding her tightly in his arms, Ellis rose swiftly to his feet. He carried her with as much ease as a rag doll, Annie thought giddily, hanging limply in his embrace. Ellis crossed through the library and foyer and strode lightly up the huge, curving staircase. Reaching the immense master bedroom, Ellis placed her gently on the king size bed, then lowered himself beside her, one thigh thrown across her legs, effectively pinning her to the bed.

His gaze was hot, triumphant, as his eyes traveled from her long hair, down the slender column of her neck, to her rounded breasts that ached for his touch. He lowered his teasing lips to one nipple, then to the other, until Annie's hands twisted frantically through his thick, black hair and she cried out her delight. But his mouth just slid lower and his hands tugged at her skirt, sliding it off her body with ease.

Then, kneeling beside her, he stripped off his own clothing with quick fluid motions. Annie marveled at the lean, tight contours of his sinewy body. His muscles tapered down his torso to the heated, hard perfection revealed to her wondering eyes. And, as he sank down beside her, stroking the satin skin of her inner thighs, waves of pulsing desire coursed through her. This magnificent man met Annie's heated response with his own and she could feel the surge of power that she was drawing from him.

Her arms tightened possessively around him. Her slender fingers stroked the taut muscles of his back, his thighs, over the sculpted curves of his hips until Ellis groaned and she felt his hot breath against her breasts.

His lips traced a path up to her mouth as he moved his rock hard body over hers, crushing her to him, taking complete and final possession of her.

They moved together, Annie spiraling upward in a new, unimagined rush of sensations. Nothing had prepared her for this kind of lovemaking. This complete surrender of the senses, with all its varied, sweet subtleties, carried an overwhelming need to be absolutely at one with her lover. As she reached the dazzling peak of her ecstasy, her cry of passion was met by his and Annie felt her universe dissolving around her.

Sometime later, Annie surfaced again, her heart beating a regular rhythm. Every fiber of her being was relaxed and all tension had drained from her body. Lying wrapped in Ellis's arms, still sensitive to every subtle nuance of his own body, she knew that he felt the same way. A small smile played around her lips as Annie, without moving Ellis's arms, reached above her head and stretched like a cat.

"Mmmmm," Ellis murmured into her neck, as his hands tightened at her waist and his lips slid down to her soft shoulders. "Where do you think you're going?"

She twisted her head to meet his lazy, contented gray eyes nose to nose.

"Nowhere," she replied promptly, running her tongue lightly over his bottom lip and snuggling closer into his warm embrace.

"Oh, Annie," he muttered against her mouth. "I knew from the moment I laid eyes on you that it could be like this with you: all that fire you keep so well hidden behind your cool, on-camera image." He kissed her deeply, running his hands across her as if they were trying to memorize every inch of her slender waist and hips. "What about you darling?" he urged. "Are you as happy as I am?"

Annie gazed up from under her lowered lashes and saw slate eyes, softened by their lovemaking, searching for an answer. A bubble of giddy amusement rose in her throat and the words came out before she had a chance to think about them. "Well..." She let the doubtful syllable drag out. "Happy?" she asked, trying to sound dubious. "I guess so..." She watched a flicker of doubt play across his chiseled features, then broke out into an irrepressible giggle. "Of course, Ellis...but ...well..." She bit softly into his shoulder. "I think I'm hungry!"

Ellis threw back his head and roared, then leaned over to her again. "Great," he leered, getting into the spirit, "but what are you hungry for?" His tongue made a tantalizing circle around one rosy nipple and Annie bit back a cry of pleasure. Suddenly, Ellis stopped and leaped off the bed.

"Where are you going?" she demanded.

"You said you were hungry," he replied, grinning. "And I try to be a gracious host." Annie started to get up but Ellis stopped her with a hand on her shoulder. "You stay here."

She shrugged and lay back down on the bed, watching Ellis stride, naked and unselfconscious, out of the bedroom. She heard him padding down the stairs as she snuggled into a pillow, bemused by the whole experience. She knew full well that she'd never before been brought to such heights of desire and fulfillment. And now that she knew what it was like, how could she go back to her peaceful, quiet existence? Annie gripped the pillow harder. No, if she was really honest, the answer was a definite no. The sparks and the conflict that she'd felt ever since she'd first encountered Ellis had led to this one, inevitable conclusion. And here, in his bed, she couldn't be less than honest about it: she wanted him, she needed him. *This* was the man she could love.

Annie felt herself blushing as Ellis returned to the room, wondering if he could read her thoughts. But, for the moment, Ellis seemed preoccupied with balancing the silver tray he carried. Annie sat up, pulling the navy blue top sheet taut across her breasts. "What's that?" she asked curiously, pointing to the tray with her free hand.

Ellis set the tray down on the antique oak nightstand and sat down beside her. As Annie surveyed the delicate china heaped with thinly sliced, honey-baked ham, Brie cheese, crackers, and olives and the silver cooler with a bottle in it, Ellis reached forward and gently tugged the sheet from her breasts.

"Beautiful," he murmured, bending down to lick each nipple just long enough to make them erect. "Still hungry?"

Annie blushed, but there was no hiding her physical response. "Yes, I am," she insisted.

"Good," Ellis replied smoothly, pulling the bottle of Dom Perignon from the cooler. "I hope you're thirsty, too. I thought this would be appropriate for a celebration." He popped the cork, which went flying across the room, and poured the foaming liquid into two Lalique champagne glasses. He handed one to Annie and lifted his glass in a toast.

"Here's to hunger," he said suggestively, touching his glass lightly against hers. "May it last forever."

Forever? Annie wondered. Did he really mean that? Annie realized that Ellis was still an enigma to her. And she didn't dare hope, quite yet, that he could've made up his mind about falling in love with her as quickly as she had. She smiled softly at him. "Yes," she replied, "I'll drink to that."

Serious thoughts disappeared, as if the warm atmosphere that pervaded the room, banished any deep considerations or worries about the future. For the moment, they were here, in Ellis's bedroom, together, in perfect union. As they dug hungrily into the food, spreading Brie on crackers and feeding the morsels to each other, they sipped champagne and gazed deeply into each other's eyes. There was no room for heavy conversation. There was instead, a feeling of ease which Annie wouldn't have traded for anything in the world. She hadn't known it was possible to feel this lighthearted and this intense at the same time. She and Ellis joked and cavorted like two kids, but, underneath the levity, was a serious and sensuous thread which made this much more than a mere kids' game.

Annie wrinkled her brow trying to think back to what Nancy had told her about Ellis. Despite his looks and charm, and despite his former entanglements, he did not have a playboy reputation. This was no guarantee for what might occur in the future, Annie realized, but it was a good sign. For the moment, she'd take it step by step.

"Why the serious look?" Ellis's husky voice broke into her thoughts and Annie realized her face must have been mirroring her emotions.

"Nothing," she stammered, then bit her lip in vexation.

Ellis put a gentle hand under her chin, forcing her to look at him. He smiled at her. "Come on, Annie," he said softly, "no more of that. We're past all the awkwardness. There's no going back." His hand slipped from her chin to the nape of her neck and, with his fingers entwined in her tangled, silky hair, he pulled her forward to meet his kiss.

No going back? she thought fleetingly. If only she knew what he meant by those words. There was no doubt in her mind that she would take the plunge with body and soul and, with her eyes, she tried to convey that to Ellis. Every caress, every kiss, every moment of passion that he gave to her, she would return in kind. Annie was willing to let their love dictate their actions and she flashed this message with her sparking, hazel eyes. Surely Ellis must be able to read her thoughts now. But as his mouth began its sensual exploration, Annie felt herself respond and all thoughts of doubt seemed to vanish from her mind.

"Oh, Ellis," she gasped, pulling her mouth from his. But he just grinned and reached to take the glass from her. As their hands met on the stem of the glass, it tilted and the champagne arced out in a glistening curve, landing in tiny droplets on Annie's stomach.

"Oh, dear," Ellis responded, in mock distress. He bent his mouth to the little pool of champagne that had formed over Annie's naval. "Let me take care of that." His tongue flicked at the little pool and he pressed his lips to her flesh, tickling her with delight. His tongue then forged lazy, voluptuons circles around her navel and Annie shivered, feeling the pangs of desire stir within her.

They played like this for what seemed like hours. Ellis gave himself as freely to her as she gave herself to him. Their sensual pleasure went beyond anything Annie had imagined possible. The bed was their home for those several hours and they never strayed from it as they nourished each other's appetites with passionate kisses and heated caresses.

His musky scent fired her deepest desires and she opened herself to him as if there were no tomorrow. Her passionate cries for fulfillment seemed to ignite a fire within Ellis and he met her every move with his own, welding their bodies and their very beings into a union of love and sensual energy.

"Annie love," Ellis murmured, enveloping her in his arms, against his expansive chest. His hands stroked and demanded. His mouth coaxed her further and further toward total abandon. "Come on, darling . . . yes . . ." his voice trailed off. "You're mine, Annie, and I'll take care of you . . . I'll always take care of you."

CHAPTER
Six

THE SUN BEAT down on Annie's bikini-clad body and she stretched contentedly in the unseasonable warm rays. The heat and sunshine combined to give her a completely langorous feeling. She turned over and reached for her suntan oil, then looked around the deck and realized Ellis was nowhere to be seen. She got up, padded to the teak railing, and peered over the side.

Just then, Ellis's head poked up from the rippling blue-green water and, gazing upward, he spotted Annie staring at him.

He removed his diving mask. "Give me a hand with these oysters, you lazy wench," he called, gesturing to the bucket he held in one hand.

Annie rested her elbow on the railing and leaned her chin into the palm of her hand. "Not till you apologize for calling me a lazy wench," she laughed down at him.

"Okay," Ellis replied obediently. "I apologize. Now get down here!"

Annie shrugged and sauntered over to the swim ladder at the stern and leaned over to take the bucket from Ellis. As she climbed back on deck, she heard Ellis behind her.

"Nice view," he remarked, staring at the curve of her hips where they funneled into the tiny slip of her shiny bikini bottom.

77

"Glad you like it," she threw back casually over her shoulder. A few intimate weeks spent with Ellis, whenever their busy schedules allowed, had only served to sharpen their appetites for each other, and Annie felt a deep relaxed sense of well-being whenever they were together. This weekend had been perfect, she reflected. They'd launched before sunset on Saturday and Ellis guided *Aurora* down the Mississippi, toward the gulf where the wide, lazy river met the sea.

They'd broiled huge, rare steaks in the galley, occasionally bumping into each other while Annie fashioned a fresh salad and dressing. After a long, lazy dinner, they'd taken their brandies on deck and settled into comfortable chairs. They gazed at the stars together as Ellis pointed out various constellations and the brightly glowing planet Venus.

Later, settled into the luxurious master stateroom, they'd made love, bringing each other to almost unbearable heights of pleasure before they drifted off to sleep. Annie had slept comfortably in Ellis's arms, secure and happy. They both awoke again and again, turning to each other, murmuring endearments, seeking that fulfilling pleasure of love over and over.

Annie was the first one to wake this morning and she was already up on deck sunning herself when Ellis appeared, still rumpled from sleep, grinning like a Chesire cat.

"Want to go diving?" he drawled.

"No," Annie had replied. "I want to get some sun."

"Okay," Ellis yawned, "have it your way. I'm an overworked physician, but I'm still willing to forage for food."

Annie laughed, remembering the well-stocked galley.

"You just have a desire for oysters, Ellis. I'd hardly put that in the foraging category."

She recalled how Ellis knelt beside her, tugging gently at her loosened top, running a possessive hand across her breasts. "No," he corrected, "there's only one thing I desire and that's right here, stretched out on the deck. I do, however, have an *urge* for oysters." And, after a brief kiss, he was over the side. She heard the sucking sound of his scuba gear and his splash as she closed her eyes and dozed lazily.

Now she peered down at the bucket he had filled and felt herself growing hungry. "I'll get started shucking these right away," she called back to Ellis as he stripped off his wet suit and tanks.

"You're not only lazy," he laughed, "you're greedy, too!" He appraised Annie's body once more. "Don't you ever worry about getting fat?"

"Absolutely not," Annie returned smugly. "I never have to worry about weight, no matter how much I eat."

"I've noticed," Ellis teased. "But I want you to come in the water for a few minutes before we start on the oysters. It's gorgeous today—crystal clear and calm. Come on, you feline, stop sleeping in the sun for a while."

Annie gazed up at the sun, then back at Ellis, as he stood dripping, tan and lean. "Okay," she agreed and climbed down the ladder to the swim step. Taking a deep breath and bracing herself for the plunge, she dove into the water in a graceful swan dive.

"Oh," she gasped as she surfaced. "Ellis, you liar, it's freezing!"

"Just wanted you to get a taste of what I've had to go through to provide you with a gourmet meal."

Annie dived down again and came up by the ladder. She grabbed Ellis by the ankle and pulled him into the water beside her. They laughed and frolicked like two carefree children, dunking and splashing each other.

They swam the length of the boat, then floated content-edly side by side.

"Mmm, this is wonderful," Annie confessed, once she'd gotten used to the temperature.

"Dare?" Ellis treaded water beside her, his gray eyes glistening mischievously.

"Dare what?" Annie asked suspiciously. She'd had occasion to learn over the past few weeks that Ellis's dares usually led to things she'd never done before.

"Come here." Ellis pulled her toward the ladder.

"Wait a second, Ellis, I didn't say I'd accepted the dare. What is it?" But Annie already knew what he had in mind as Ellis reached behind her and untied the string to her bikini top. "Hey, stop it," she protested, holding the flimsy little top to her breasts.

"Don't you want to swim nude?" Ellis's eyes were full of mischief.

"Not here," Annie retorted, looking around. In point of fact, she'd never done any such thing anywhere.

"Why not?" Ellis gestured expansively. "There's no one around."

He was right, Annie thought. They'd moored for the night in a secluded cove and all around them were trees festooned with hanging Spanish moss, filled with exotic birds crying out across the water. Little animals darted through the thick undergrowth on shore but there were no people.

"You first," she countered and Ellis immediately pulled off his brief, tight trunks while staring at her challengingly. It was maddening, Annie thought, as she draped the bikini top over the lowest rung of the swim ladder. He always managed to coax her into some kind of outrageous behavior. She giggled as Ellis swam around her then reached out and pulled at her little bikini bottom until it slid down her thighs and off. The im-mediate sensation of being nude in the water was rather strange to Annie but as she and Ellis began to cavort around, it seemed like the most natural thing in the world. The cold water slid deliciously all over her and she wondered why bathing suits had ever been invented.

Out of breath, Annie swam back to the ladder and clung to it for a rest. Ellis surfaced in front of her, backing Annie up against the stern of the boat, his arms encircling her. When he kissed her, Annie felt the ladder's metal rungs pressing into the small of her back and she squirmed protestingly. She pressed herself against the length of Ellis's wet, naked body. She felt her breathing grow rapid as she gazed at his dripping muscular arms, then up, into his smoky gaze.

"Ellis," she protested weakly as he deftly parted her thighs with his own.

"Don't you want me, Annie?" Ellis asked in a breathy, teasing voice. With an arm encircling the firm curve of her hips, he drew her up to his heated strength. The water rendered Annie weightless and with her legs, she encircled his waist and her arms went around his neck. In the crystal water of the secluded cove, Annie and her lover moved together, floating in this sea of bliss.

Much later, after a dinner of steamed oysters, dipped in melted butter and lemon and accompanied by a bottle of chilled white wine, they cruised back to New Orleans through the sunset. After they moored the cruiser in its slip, Annie snuggled tiredly into the Jaguar's leather seat and Ellis drove her to her apartment.

"Want me to come up?" he asked.

"No, Ellis," Annie replied, stifling a yawn. "I've got to be at the station early tomorrow. Special report to do."

"All right, darling." He leaned over and kissed her tenderly. "But don't forget about dinner tomorrow night. It's important."

"Oh?" Annie's hazel eyes widened.

"It will be a month to the day since we met," Ellis reminded her. "I think it's time we discussed our future."

Annie's heart skipped a beat. She hadn't counted the days they'd been together and she was surprised to find that Ellis had. Her feelings for him had deepened far beyond the first time they had made love. Now she knew for certain that this was the only man for her—the only man there would ever be. She wanted to spend the rest of her life with Ellis, to marry him, to be with him always. But she'd been content to give him the time he needed to sort out his feelings. She knew, of course, that she meant a lot to him. He'd proven in a dozen ways that he was no casual taker. But she hadn't dared hope that he could fall in love as deeply, or as quickly, as she had.

"Tomorrow," she replied, sliding out of the car.

Back in her apartment, Annie prepared her clothes for the next day's work, then sank onto the couch, reflecting on Ellis's words. The mere thought of what lay ahead sent shivers of anticipation running up her spine. It had been the most exciting, the most wonderful few weeks of her life, she thought. He seemed to be able to bring out all the playfulness in her nature and all the tenderness as well.

They'd strolled hand in hand through the French Quarter, Annie marveling at Ellis's eye for beautiful art and architecture. He pointed out styles and buildings, explained their origins and allowed her to expand her own vision of the lovely city. Together they'd listened to jazz and gone dancing at an old luxury hotel which featured a big band sound. As Annie was swept round the floor in Ellis's arms, to a 1940s tempo, she'd felt like a heroine in an old movie and she'd loved it. They'd discussed Mardi Gras, each teasingly keeping their planned costumes a secret from the other.

It was all as close to idyllic as she could have ever imagined, and she felt like a flower, opening under his expert cultivation. For the first time in years, Annie's defenses were down and she was glad about it. It was wonderful to feel so open, so free, and so in love. Where it would lead was a question that might be answered tomorrow night. Ellis certainly acted as if he was in love with her, although he had never put it into words, and Annie realized how much she did want to hear him say it. She'd committed herself, body and soul, and surely Ellis must know that by now. Her marriage had never been what this intense, passionate love affair had become. And she knew now that she'd been right the first time they'd made love: there would never be any going back. She was his forever. The only nagging worry she had was the prospect of Ellis's taking a position at Johns Hopkins. He'd mentioned it once or twice in passing but hadn't really discussed the subject with her. And Annie, in turn, hadn't pried.

Annie shook herself out of her reverie and prepared for bed. Despite her excitement and anticipation, the swimming and sunning had taken their toll on her. Even thinking about tomorrow night couldn't keep her awake but her last thought as she drifted off to sleep, snuggled under the comforter, was of the promise in Ellis's eyes.

"Hey, Carroll," Rudy called out cheerfully as Annie headed for her office, "have a nice weekend?"

"Wonderful," Annie replied, smiling.

"Do I detect a certain radiance?"

"Rudy!" Annie admonished, feeling slightly embarrassed.

"Well, he's right," David's voice came from directly behind her and Annie swung around to see the blond news director grinning down at her. "That certain . . . *je ne sais quoi . . .* " he said as he studied her flushing face for a moment. "Hey, look—freckles! Been out in the sun, Annie? Maybe on somebody's yacht?"

Annie sputtered angrily, then gave up and laughed with the rest of them. It was impossible to keep anything from these people who, after all, were all paid to be skilled observers. But it was downright embarrassing to have your private life absolutely exposed under the searchlights of their amused gazes.

Annie composed herself. "It was a lovely weekend, David," she said with a straight face. "And for all you know, I could have gotten these freckles by sitting out on my patio. It was hot all weekend!"

"Have it your way." David shrugged, but his smile told her that he wasn't fooled in the least.

"Have I got anything after the Mardi Gras float story?" Annie asked to change the subject.

"That was moved back," Monica called out, hurrying over with Annie's coffee. "You've got staff meeting this morning. The float stories are going to be in the afternoon."

Annie groaned, taking the coffee from Monica. "Have you called the float sponsors to make sure we can re-schedule?"

"Yeah, it's okay with all of them except the building contractors group. That's, uh, wait a second," Monica scanned down the list she was carrying, "oh, right, the giant tools with the 'scantily clad' models perched on top."

Annie laughed. "I think we'll live without that one. We've still got all the traditional ones: the devils and the voodoo floats?"

"Uh-huh, no problem with anyone else?" Monica queried.

"No . . ." Annie thought a moment. "Wait . . . I've got

an idea, Monica. See if you can get in touch with anyone from the Cathedral Committee. They're supposed to be doing a gorgeous religious float. If it'll be completed this afternoon, we can use it to fill in the slot we originally planned for the construction float. Seems more appropriate anyway."

"Right." Monica hurried off.

"Good thinking," David said admiringly.

"What's up, David? What's the staff meeting about?"

"Sponsors are acting up again. Got to make some on-the-air policy changes."

"Honestly." Annie's voice was exasperated. "Don't they ever let up?"

"Nope," David answered calmly. "If they didn't keep bothering us, they'd feel like they weren't getting their money's worth."

"Why don't they just check their sales' charts?"

"Don't waste your sarcasm on me," David laughed, "and don't be so logical—this is entertainment."

"It is *not*. It's the news," Annie began, then smiled. "Don't tease me, David, not so early in the day. Honestly, though, you'd think they had better things to do than hassle poor, harried, overworked news teams."

"Come on, Annie, you know the customer is always right."

"I know," she sighed, "but that doesn't mean I have to like it."

David checked his watch. "Got to make a few calls before the meeting," he said. "See you in the conference room at eleven."

"Annie, it's all set for the Cathedral Committee float." Monica said. "They'll be done just about when you're through with the other ones."

"Terrific." Annie smiled at Monica. "I think I'll write my intro now, before the conference. It sounds like I'm going to be pressed for time when the broadcast rolls around."

"Okay," Monica said cheerfully. "I'll call you when it's time for the conference."

"Thanks." Annie replied, settling herself at the typewriter. She managed to get an entire rough draft done before Monica buzzed and sent her on her way to the meeting. But, despite her resolve to focus her thoughts on work, Annie found it harder than usual to concentrate. Her mind kept drifting to the evening and her anticipation of what Ellis would say.

After the predictably boring meeting, Annie hunted up Rudy and Joe.

"Looking for someone?" Joe's voice came from behind her and she saw the irrepressible twosome poking their heads out of an editing room.

"We're ready," Rudy chimed in. *"We've* been ready since this morning."

"Don't," Annie groaned. "It's not my fault that the staff meeting was called. I haven't even had lunch!"

"Well, get your stuff and let's move it. We'll pick up some fast food on the way to the floats," Joe offered.

"Bless you," Annie said fervently. Jogging to her office to grab her purse, notebook, and makeup bag, she joined Rudy and Joe on the way to the van. "I'm all set."

Twenty minutes later, Annie tossed the remains of a terrible hamburger into a paper bag in the van. Then she hastily checked her makeup, retied the silk scarf she wore around her neck, and pinned her long hair, hoping it would stay up for a change. Rudy and Joe, as usual, concentrated on card playing, giving only occasional thoughts to Rudy's driving.

It was a whirlwind afternoon, the threesome traveling around from site to site, where the different floats were being elaborately constructed from papier-mâché, flowers, and even aluminum foil. Annie talked to creators, sponsors, builders, one after another while Joe alternated coverage of her talking with shots of the many floats. Between interviews, the two crewmen flirted and joked with the lovely, sometimes barely clad, girls who obligingly posed in their provocative theme costumes atop the various floats.

The last stop was at the Cathedral Committee float. It was less frivolous than the others due to its religious tone.

Annie admired the skill which had gone into planning and building the colorful and faithful reproduction of the Cathedral at Chartres—complete with elaborate stained-glass-looking windows, only these windows were made of thousands of flower petals, nearly as vibrant and colorful as the originals. It was a great contrast to the other floats and a perfect way to wind up the coverage.

Back at the station, Annie told Joe and Rudy her ideas on assembling the footage they'd filmed and recorded. They agreed, with a few minor changes, and headed off to an editing room. Annie took her rough draft introduction and polished it up with some minimal rewriting. This certainly wouldn't be an earthshaking news story, she thought, but the piece should look pretty good. She got up from her typewriter and headed off for the editing rooms.

"That's some float," David exclaimed as Annie huddled next to him in front of a flatbed editing machine. "What a beauty."

"David," she chimed in sarcastically, *"that* happens to be a girl, wearing practically nothing, on top of that float! Don't try and pass it off as a compliment to the float. And," she added, "enough of those skimpy costumes, put more shots of the floats into it."

"Killjoy," Rudy grumbled goodnaturedly as he looked

over her shoulder at the images on the viewing screen in the middle of the editing table.

"Listen, I don't care if you want to save all the 'good' shots and splice them together so you *boys* can enjoy them later, but that's not what's going out on the air," Annie said firmly.

"We know that, we were just having fun," Joe butted in, trying to sound hurt.

Annie laughed. "Come on, let's get it together."

"It is, Annie," David said, amused. "We were just teasing you, the stuff we're really using is already spliced together on this roll." He handed it to Joe, who threaded it into the editing machine.

As Annie stared at the images flashing across the viewer, her assessment of the assignment proved correct. The story was upbeat and colorful and had captured the air of mounting excitement which the approach of Carnival always engendered in New Orleans. Annie had coaxed good statements from even the least articulate of the float people and the results were light and pleasing.

"My, Annie," David remarked slyly, in response to a closeup. "Relaxing in the sun has given you a bit of color. It seems to have done you a world of good."

Objectively, she supposed, looking at the film in front of her, she *did* look good. It was difficult to pinpoint the difference but there was definitely something new coming across these days.

"I personally always thought the boss lady was gorgeous," Rudy said, smugly. "Didn't I, Joe?"

Joe offered his own assessment. "Yeah," he drawled, "but you gotta admit, our Miss Carroll's flashing something special these days."

"Glad you guys approve," Annie quipped. She knew her only defense against this merciless teasing was in joking right back. "Say, David, that gives me an idea."

She turned toward the grinning news director. "If all you guys are seeing so much difference in me lately, I guess the audience sees it too and it's probably reflected in the ratings, don't you think?" Before David had a chance to reply, Annie hurried on. "So, what I was thinking..." she paused for effect, "if the ratings are going up, it seems to me that I ought to be getting a substantial raise. Don't you agree?"

David groaned in reply. "We'll have to see the ratings first," he said cautiously.

"Oh, come now, David..." Annie tried not to laugh. "After all, you're the one who keeps telling me how 'marvelous' and 'glowing' I've been looking..."

Joe started whistling "As Time Goes By" and all four of them dissolved into laughter.

"Let me see your copy," David said as he flicked on the lights and the foursome began to go their seperate ways.

"It's in my office." Annie walked with David across the newsroom floor. As she neared her cubicle, Monica called out to her, "Phone, Annie."

Annie moved behind her desk, handing the copy of her story to David with one hand and picking up the receiver with the other.

"Anne Carroll," she said briskly.

"Hi, darling." Even through the phone Ellis's voice sounded distressed.

"Hello." Annie smiled.

"Annie, listen, I'm apologizing in advance. I can't tell you how sorry I am but I've got to cancel out on dinner tonight."

A wave of disappointment swept over Annie and she sank heavily into her chair. "What's wrong?" she asked calmly trying not to sound upset.

"I... Annie, I can't really talk about it right now."

Ellis sounded strange, pressured. It was a tone she'd never before heard in his voice and she realized that it wouldn't help him any if she got angry or hurt over this. But, she thought, why tonight of all nights?

"All right, Ellis," she said softly.

He knew her too well to mistake even the smallest tinge of sorrow in her voice. "Look, darling, you must know that I wouldn't let just anything keep me away from you." He sounded concerned. "It's just that something terribly important—and unexpected—has come up. Something I have to deal with right away, before it's too late."

Too late? Annie wondered. She forced herself to sound at ease. "It's all right, Ellis," she said firmly. "Whatever it is. I'll grab a bite to eat and be home later if you need to reach me."

"Good." Ellis's voice was businesslike now. "I'll talk to you as soon as possible. Bye, Annie."

Annie set the receiver back in the cradle, her curiosity piqued by his vagueness. Suddenly, she started to feel sorry for herself. This certainly wasn't how she'd pictured this evening would turn out. She sighed and looked up to find David, copy still in hand, staring at her.

"Sorry," he said quietly, "I didn't mean to eavesdrop."

Annie shrugged. "It's okay," she said. "No big deal."

David's steady blue gaze surveyed her open face and saw the disappointment there. "Don't look so sad," he coaxed. "Tell you what, Annie, I'll take you to dinner after the national news is over. I'll have to be back at the station early but let's just go someplace quiet and cheerful and relax a little. Okay?"

"I don't know," Annie said shaking her head. "I think I'll just go on home."

"C'mon," he insisted. "It sounds like Ellis is tied up with something and there's no reason for you to sit home alone, getting upset. We'll go to dinner."

Annie smiled up at him. What a dear friend David could be. And he was right. "Okay," she decided. "We'll go."

A few hours later, Annie straightened her desk and checked the calendar for tomorrow's schedule. She wondered again what business Ellis had been referring to when he canceled their date, then put the thought out of her head, realizing she'd simply have to wait to hear it from Ellis himself. She headed for the ladies' room to freshen up.

When she returned to her office, David was waiting for her, his sports jacket flung over his shoulder. "Ready?" he asked and Annie nodded, smiling.

"There's a terrific little French bistro that opened up in the Quarter a few months ago—La Vie en Rose— ever been there?" he asked as he guided Annie into his black Mercedes.

"No, but I've heard about it."

"Let's go there, I think you'll like it." David made a U turn and headed toward the French Quarter.

"Don't we need reservations?" she asked dubiously. La Vie en Rose had already garnered quite a reputation in New Orleans.

"Not on a Monday night." David grinned over at her. "Besides, they know me."

This shouldn't have surprised her but the way David related to everyone at work, like just one of the guys, made it hard to realize he was a well-known member of one of New Orleans' "old families." He'd be recognized just about anywhere.

The valet took the car and David opened the heavy oak door for her. As Annie stood just inside the entry, her eyes adjusting to the dim light, David moved ahead of her to the maître'd and started to say something. Then he turned abruptly, taking Annie's arm.

"Where are we going?" she asked, startled by his sudden action.

"I just changed my mind. All of a sudden, I've got a terrific craving for Creole food," David announced as he turned her toward the door.

"But David," Annie protested, craning her head back over her shoulder, the restaurant seemed charming and elegant. It was all plants and white linen and crystal and it smelled divine. What on earth had come over David?

Suddenly, Annie's attention focused on a corner table and she knew why David had steered her away so abruptly. Even in the shadows, there was no mistaking the dark haired man who sat concentrating on his beautiful blond companion.

Annie shook her head, trying to make the picture disappear, but the image remained. It was Ellis. And across the little, intimate table, was Camille Du Maurier. She looked exquisite, but she was also obviously upset and her slender hands were held out toward Ellis, as if she was imploring him to do something. As Annie stood frozen, watching in disbelief, Ellis reached across the table and took Camille's small hands in his own. It was a gesture of intimacy that couldn't be mistaken.

"Annie," David's voice was very quiet, "let's go."

Stunned, Annie just nodded. It was a shock. She didn't really feel anything . . . yet. She tried not to think about it. She just wanted to get out of there.

Then Ellis's uncanny ability to hone in on her presence made him look up. His dark head turned in Annie's direction and his gaze wandered right to where she stood, rooted to the spot. His eyes widened in startled recognition. As their eyes met, Annie knew she couldn't maintain her composure any longer. Before Ellis could see the tears starting to well up in her eyes, she gave him a curt nod and turned toward the door.

CHAPTER

Seven

ANNIE KEPT HER face turned away from David as he steered her gently toward a quiet, low-key bar, nestled inconspicuously between two brightly-lit storefronts. Despite her controlled composure, she was sure he'd be able to see the hurt in her eyes and her tightly clenched jaw as she fought back the tears.

While David chose a secluded booth and ordered for both of them, Annie couldn't suppress the jumbled thoughts swirling around in her mind. The shock was already wearing off, and the image of Camille's intimate gaze leveled at Ellis's consoling eyes wrenched at Annie's insides like a huge claw. Annie looked around the small bar, trying to focus on something, anything that would drive the haunting picture away. But again and again, she saw Ellis's strong hands clutched around Camille's delicate white fingers—the same way he had held Annie's hands.

Then the flood that she wanted so desperately to avoid suddenly just poured out of her. For a few moments Annie cried freely, as if she might purge the painful image in a cleansing flow of tears. But, just as suddenly, she pulled herself together, working to clear her head, using a tissue to dab away the warm tears. The handkerchief David offered was no longer necessary, but the brandy the cocktail waitress had set on the table before her certainly was. Annie grasped the snifter and downed the amber liquid. The quick, warming sensation as the brandy went down served its intended purpose; with a wave of his hand, David signaled the waitress for another round.

Finally, with the immediate shock of having seen Ellis with Camille temporarily soothed by the combination of brandy and Annie's willpower, she turned to David.

"I didn't mean to break down like that, David. I . . . I just couldn't help it."

"It's all right Annie. Tears are nothing to be ashamed of." David placed a gentle, reassuring hand on Annie's shoulder.

"I feel so foolish," Annie continued. "I should have known that it wasn't over between them. Here I am, naïve enough to think Ellis, with his sweet talk, actually meant it about not having casual affairs. What a fool I was!"

Before David could reply, Annie's brow knit in angry frustration, and she continued, "You know, I think I could almost accept that Ellis is still involved with Camille, but what really burns me up is that he *lied* to me. Business he said . . . That's what he calls business?" She slammed down the second little snifter, nearly breaking it.

"Well, maybe that's exactly what it is," David offered.

"What does *that* mean?" Annie fired back.

"Camille is the daughter of a very powerful political figure, Annie. Senator Jaynes has a lot to say about a lot of things, including who may or may not get appointed to a certain prestigious position at Johns Hopkins."

Annie's lips curled sarcastically, and she almost spat her reply. "You mean the brilliant surgeon isn't above romancing a politician's daughter just to enhance his career?"

"I generally give Ellis more credit than that, Annie," David said calmly. "But you never really know. He certainly wouldn't be the first to fall off his white horse."

Once again the claw wrenched at Annie's insides. Her lips began to quiver, and she was afraid she might break down once again. Could Ellis really be that mercenary, that power hungry? And what did that make Annie to him then, other than a momentary diversion? Her love for him, the intimate words they'd shared must've meant nothing to him at all.

Straining to keep her voice steady, Annie pulled her jacket tight and turned to David. "Look, David, I'm sorry, but would you mind if I just went home now? I don't feel too well."

David stood and took Annie's hand. "Not at all," he said understandingly, "but let me drive you."

"No, that's all right. I'll take a taxi," she replied, "I'd like to be alone."

With a warm, firm grasp, David silently let her know that he was there if she needed him. Forcing a tiny smile, Annie left the bar and hailed a passing cab.

Once inside her apartment, the weight of the evening's experiences finally settled heavily on Annie's shoulders. She thought about fixing a pot of tea, maybe curling up in front of the television. But it was no good, she was too restless. Everywhere she looked, the painful images returned, clouding her eyes and her heart.

She must be strong, Annie repeated to herself as she paced around the apartment. She tried to convince herself that this was different than her marriage—this wasn't the same as when Gordon had cast her aside for the boss's daughter. Although, she thought bitterly, the similarities were striking. But she had handled that, and she would somehow handle this shock, too. Still, all her logic and determination didn't soften the emotional impact of the blow. Perhaps a shower would help soothe her feelings, help wash away the memory.

The hot water cascaded down over Annie's tear-stained cheeks, warming and massaging as it coursed across her shoulders, down the sides of her breasts in rivulets, and streaked over her thighs down into the drain. The rising steam seemed like a fog shrouding her in a protective cocoon all her own. For a while, she managed to relax and enjoy the solitude and the comforting warmth. Could her troubles simply flow down the drain like so much water, she mused.

Stepping out of the shower, finally, and wrapping herself in a soft, enveloping bath towel, Annie felt a little better. Maybe she'd have that cup of tea, after all.

Padding on bare feet into the kitchen, Annie filled her kettle and set it on the lit stove. Back in the bedroom, she rubbed vigorously with the towel, buffing her soft skin to a pink glow. Suddenly, physical memories of Ellis flooded her. She couldn't help thinking of lying nude alongside him. The memory of his arms encircling her slender waist, of his hands moving slowly across her breasts, his tanned cheeks sensually grazing her stomach—how would she ever forget him? Her heart and soul ached and she felt empty inside. Stop it, she ordered herself—it will pass. She would not dwell on the memories, and the sooner she forgot Ellis, the better.

Annie reached for a robe, and, out of the corner of her eye, spotted the little black and white photograph that Ellis had given her. Hanging innocently on the wall near the bed, the picture was an instant reminder of a love that might have been, should have been, perfect. Annie's knees weakened at the sight of it, and she collapsed onto the bed and sobbed. She found there was no way to stop her heart from pouring out its misery. Curling into a fetal position, Annie, tormented and miserable, cried herself into a fitful sleep.

The ringing telephone went off like an explosion in Annie's head, wrenching her from a troubled sleep. Still lying on top of her now-rumpled comforter, Annie reached dazedly across the bed for the phone, noting that her small quartz alarm clock read 2 A.M. She'd slept only a few hours. She could hear the whistling kettle, now reduced to a feeble whine.

Pulling the receiver to her ear, Annie didn't have a chance to speak before the familiar voice fell on her like a cold wind.

"Annie, it's me, Ellis."

She said nothing in reply, fighting the urge to scream her fury out at him, or simply hang up.

"Look, I know it's late, Annie, but I had to talk to you . . . Annie? Are you there?" Ellis's voice was as unsettling as ever.

Resisting the impulse to let the receiver drop on the floor, Annie spoke coolly. "Just a minute, Ellis, I've got to turn off the stove." Setting the receiver down, she walked into the kitchen and turned off the stove. The momentary delay was just enough time for her to become fully awake and regain her composure. She returned to the bedroom and reached purposefully for the phone.

In an acidic tone, she spoke calmly into the receiver. "Okay, Ellis. Now that you woke me up, what do you want?"

"Annie! You were asleep with the stove on? That's dangerous. Are you all right?"

The note of genuine concern in Ellis's voice was momentarily disarming, but Annie gripped the receiver and retorted, "Look, Ellis, I haven't the time or the patience to play twenty questions with you at two in the morning. What do you want?"

"You're right, Annie. I just wanted to..."

But before he could finish the sentence, Annie's temper got the better of her. "Wanted to what?" she fired at him. "Wanted to explain why you lied to me?"

"I didn't lie to you, Annie."

"Then what would you call it? Look, if you're involved with Camille, then you had no business stringing me along." The bitter words burned as they poured from her throat.

"Annie, I didn't string you along, and I'm not involved with Camille." Ellis's voice was firm.

Annie found she wanted desperately to believe him. But she'd believed him before, and the recurring image of that intimate restaurant scene was not going to disappear easily.

"Then what were the two of you doing together, after you said you had a business meeting?"

The silence on the other end of the line only served to confirm her deepest fears. After a few moments, he responded. "I know you're upset, Annie, but pointless arguing will get us nowhere. Let me come over and we can work it out together. You *must* trust me. I simply cannot give you an explanation yet, but there *is* one. After what we've been to each other, I think I deserve something more than this kind of reaction from you."

Annie saw red. How dare he turn the tables like this, make it seem like *her* fault? "Forget it!" she spat out. "And forget me. It's finished!"

"Annie, wait, don't hang up," he insisted.

"Ellis, it's late. I'm tired and I have nothing more to say to you. I've got work in the morning, so, if you don't mind, *Doctor*..."

"I do mind!" Ellis retorted unexpectedly, a new edge of anger in his voice. "This is ridiculous! I can't believe how incredibly mistrustful you are, Annie. Why the hell won't you just accept the fact that there is an explanation, a very innocent one, as a matter of fact! And that I'm quite simply not at liberty to reveal it right now!"

Annie was taken aback by his unexpected vehemence. Perhaps, she thought unwillingly, he really was telling the truth. But, then, why all the secrecy? No, she thought, she couldn't just sit back and take his proclamations of honesty at face value. There was simply too much in her own past experience which wouldn't allow that to happen.

"Ellis," she began, "I'd like to believe you, I really would. But all this vagueness, all this secrecy...How do you expect me to feel about it? Be honest, Ellis. If the tables were turned, how would you feel?"

"I hope I'd be a hell of a lot more understanding— and trusting—than you are," he replied soberly. "I don't think I'd just condemn you out of hand for something I didn't understand. At least, I'd give you the chance to prove you weren't doing anything wrong or underhanded!"

Annie was stung by the restrained anger in his voice, and her temper flared in self-defense. "I thought I'd made it perfectly clear, Ellis, that you *do* have the chance to prove that you weren't doing anything, as you say, 'wrong or underhanded.' And unless I've been hearing wrong during this entire, fruitless conversation, it seems to me that you've consistently refused to clear yourself!"

There was a pause at the other end of the line, then Ellis responded. "I will...in time. Why don't you believe that?"

"Maybe it's because it's too familiar a line. And these

particular circumstances are a bit on the repetitive side, too," Annie spat without thinking.

"What are you talking about?" Ellis sounded confused.

Annie bit her lip, wishing fervently that those last words had never been spoken. But it was too late now, she realized.

"I'm talking about something that happened to me a long time ago," she said coldly. "I shouldn't have brought it up at all, since it doesn't really involve you and me. But..."

"But, obviously, it made an indelible impression on you," Ellis cut in.

"Don't play drugstore psychologist with me!" Annie snapped. "You're specialty is the *heart,* not the mind, and it seems to me that you're not doing too well in your own field of expertise right now!"

"All I meant, Annie, was that I wish something from your past wasn't creating these feelings about me... about us. It isn't fair..."

"Our respective pasts just seem to keep cropping up and getting in the way, don't they, Ellis?" Annie asked sarcastically.

"I'll ignore the implications of that. Now, will you calm down and tell me exactly what it is that you're talking about?"

"I've never said very much to you about my marriage," Annie began, in a hurry now just to get the explanation of her hasty words over with. "But, obviously, it didn't turn out to be, as they say, 'made in heaven.' That's putting it mildly." Annie paused and took a breath. "Anyway, Gordon—my ex-husband—managed to surprise the hell out of me. I thought I'd married a serious, dedicated law student who would use his training to take up causes, issues which are important. As it turned out, what I had really married was a very ambitious, very manipulative subhuman who gave me the honor of putting him through law school—and then set his sights on a cushy private position in the private sector, with all the attendant opportunities and benefits. Including the quickest guaranteed path to the top . . . called the boss's daughter!"

Ellis seized the pause. "I'm sorry, Annie. Very sorry. I didn't know any of that, but it does explain, to some extent, why you'd leap to conclusions about . . ."

"Don't you use that patronizing tone with me," Annie broke in warningly.

"Well, don't compare me to your ex-husband!" Ellis retorted. "History *doesn't* repeat. This isn't the same thing at all—only the most superficial veneer of the situation is similar."

"Are you implying that I'm superficial?" Annie asked caustically.

"Stop twisting my words around," Ellis said, his voice barely controlled. "And stop confusing me and what we have with something that happened to you years ago. Or," he continued, his tone ominous, "am I to take it that you really *believe* that this is some kind of not-so-instant replay in your life?"

The warning note in Ellis's voice was perfectly clear. Annie knew that he didn't want to hear that she'd been thrown into this state because she, realistically, felt he was anything like Gordon. And, to be fair, she had believed that Ellis *was* different. Otherwise, she would never have let her guard down and become involved with him in the first place. But it was hard to forget completely the lessons which were so bitterly engraved on her heart. And it was hard, too, to ignore the similarities in the situations.

But, Annie reasoned to herself, she'd given him every

opportunity to explain his actions. She'd even broke down and opened up to him about a chapter in her own emotional history which was still painful to contemplate. Now Ellis knew: he knew what had happened to her marriage, he knew where the scars came from, and he knew—he must know—how she felt about him. And still, he was offering no explanations, only shallow psychology and vague reassurances.

Annie's pride arose. "I don't think this is any kind of instant replay," she said coolly. "But I don't hear anything coming from you which gives me any reason to believe you, either." She paused, giving him one last chance to explain, but he didn't say anything at all. "So," she continued, in a frigid tone, "I really don't see the point of continuing this conversation. It seems to be going around in circles...and I'm tired." She took a breath. "I'll talk to you sometime, Ellis..."

"Annie, wait," he said, and her heart fluttered. But Ellis's next words were not what she wanted to hear. "I...well, maybe we just need a few days to calm down. About Mardi Gras...we had a date. I'd like it very much if you'd let me take you out for the evening as we planned." Ellis's voice was sober.

Annie wanted desperately to say yes, to forget what had happened, but it was impossible. "No, Ellis," she replied firmly. "I don't think it would be wise for either one of us. You just go on and have a good time without me."

"I'm not sure I can do that," he said. "I understand that you're terribly confused by what's going on, but can't you put it out of your mind, just for one evening? After all, I don't want you to have to miss out on such a gala night and all we'd planned."

Annie set her lips in a firm line. "I don't plan to *miss*

out on anything," she replied, "so don't bother worrying about me."

"Oh," came Ellis's flat reply. "In that case, I hope you enjoy yourself," he said stiffly.

"I'm sure I will," Annie replied with forced lightness. Then, before she could change her mind, she hung up the phone receiver, wondering at the same time if this would be the last time she'd ever talk with Ellis.

CHAPTER

Eight

THE FULL-LENGTH MIRROR on the armoire reflected an exotic Arabian harem girl, and Annie stared at her image in amused surprise. Used to thinking of herself as sporting a very professional, rather conventional career-girl look, she would never have believed she could look so sensual and alluring as she appeared in the filmy, diaphanous Mardi Gras costume.

The outfit was extremely bold, Annie mused, but that was how she wanted to feel right now. What better way for a woman to bolster her confidence and renew her pride than to present the world with a look of mystery and beauty? Whatever intrigue the little veil across her nose added by hiding all but her flashing hazel eyes, the rest of her costume took another step further.

The silky, translucent blouse she'd fashioned was cut low and daringly revealing. Annie had considered wearing a bra the minute she saw it on. But now, noting the way the material outlined, without really detailing her rounded breasts, Annie decided to go natural. The nearly sheer fabric had a magic all its own, and she swayed within its folds, feeling a sense of freedom and release. The sequined sash around her waist pulled the blouse close to her taut stomach, funneling the sensual top down into a slim waistline, and accentuating the slight, curvy flair of her hips. The loose pantaloons which draped her legs were almost as sheer as the blouse. They ballooned over her knees, and gathered below her calves. Annie's slim legs flashed through the material, from high on her thighs down to her slender, pretty ankles. Standing with her hand on her hip, Annie flexed her calf muscles as she touched a brightly painted toe to the floor and arched her ankle upward. Little left to the imagination here, she thought, but she was pleased with the effect. She would have loved to go barefoot, but the gold lamé sandals with their slender spaghetti straps were nearly as good.

She purposely left her head uncovered and her long hair down; and her chestnut locks gleamed and flowed freely as she turned her head back and forth, wondering at this liberated version of a sheik's pride. Annie pulled on the green satin jerkin-like vest which completed the outfit, and giggled a little. She could just imagine a traditional, conservative sheik, and how he would explode if he ever saw one of his wives in such a revealing outfit. It *was* a bit risqué, she thought. But more important, it made her feel daring, defiant, and ready to make the most of this, the biggest of all evenings in old New Orleans.

Annie removed the little veil and went to her makeup mirror to add more blusher to her cheeks. As she scrutinized the finished product, Annie sighed. Although her spirits were too high for her to bemoan the fact that she wasn't with Ellis, she was disappointed nevertheless that he would not see her in this alluring costume. Camille Du Maurier had nothing on her, Annie reflected with pride, and if Ellis could see her now, he'd realize just what he'd lost.

Annie's confidence continued to rise as she stared at her bright features. Was this the same woman who had come from St. Louis to New Orleans to forget a bad and painful marriage? Appraising her youthful, yet womanly, countenance, she honestly could not see worry lines, or the usual scars of a broken heart. Of course, the experiences of two disappointing romances were etched deeply into her mental diary. She hoped any emotional scars she carried from the latest hurt would be fully concealed behind the little veil, and she draped it back in place.

As Annie fastened a few layers of thin gold chains around her slender throat, she wondered what she would do if she drew the attention of someone new tonight. There would no doubt be scores of elligible males at the various parties, and her femininity, so lavishly revealed, would turn at least a few heads. But the thought of getting involved with a man seemed as dismal as it was unlikely. After her recent heartbreak, Annie could not see herself in that vulnerable situation again. At least not for a long, long while.

She reached for one of her favorite fragrances, and with the tiny stopper of her crystal perfume decanter, Annie dabbed some of the scent behind her ears, on her wrists, and down the V of her blouse across her cleavage. It was not the scent she knew Ellis liked—that would bring back too many painful memories. As Annie continued her reverie, the movement of her costume's silky fabric across her flesh sent a mild shiver through her, filling her with fleeting images of masculine hands stroking her, of a man's arm encircling her waist, drawing her hips to his. Then, vexed, she stopped her musings as she realized that these were no thoughts of some imaginary creature, but memories of Ellis. For a moment, there had been an ache of desire, but Annie fought the memories, and suppressed her feelings of loss.

She was determined not to give in to his haunting image. It would never do. If she was going to have a good time tonight, Annie knew she had to brush the past aside and hold her head up high. It might not be easy, but, she reminded herself, she was used to difficult times. She'd been through them before. This was Carnival, and she was committed to enjoying herself, despite Ellis. Besides, with her veil in place to hide any lapse in her determination, she was sure she could pull it off. To anyone taking the time to pay attention to her, Annie would appear confident and vibrant. Whatever they suspected was contained in the features behind her veil, whether pain, sorrow, or unbridled joy, it would just have to remain an exotic mystery.

The doorbell rang, and Annie, torn from her musings, realized that it must be David. A quick, final check through her armoire confirmed that nothing she owned would go with her outfit. Grabbing a thin crocheted shawl, she shut the mirrored door and went to answer the bell.

When she opened the door, there, lounging in the door frame was a hideous ghoul, its fangs dripping red, a livid scar running down one cheek, and a single bulging eye on one side of the putrid green face. Annie was taken aback until she saw the creature stuffing a familiar pipe with tobacco and raising it to it's mouth. Then she broke into a wide grin.

"Well, what do you think?" David's familiar voice came from behind the obviously corny mask.

Annie laughed. "David, you look simply terrible!" she said, as she fastened her circle of keys onto her belt and headed out the door.

"Hold on a moment," David said, taking Annie's arm and halting her movements. Then, standing at arm's length, he gave her an attentive up-and-down scrutiny, and uttered a grunt of approval. "That's some costume, Annie. I think I should've brought a flaming torch to

beat back the wolves that'll be trailing us all over town!"
Annie's blush was her only answer as they turned and
continued out into the streets to the waiting cab.

The streets of New Orleans were literally swelling
with people starting their Mardi Gras celebrations. Costumed figures were everywhere and throngs of revelers
were pouring in and out of the town's many clubs and
restaurants. As the kinetic energy of the celebrants
charged the air with excitement, Annie felt more free
and at ease than she had in days. Music seemed to fill
the air, and a warm evening breeze blew lightly through
her costume, adding to her brimming anticipation of the
evening's delights.

A distant blast from the horn of the magnificent stern-
wheeled steamer, *Delta Queen,* added to the atmosphere
and Annie imagined the graceful riverboat carrying the
usual load of tourists and sightseers along the mighty
Mississippi. As the cab crawled down renowned Saint
Charles Avenue, it passed a trolley car, and Annie stared
in amusement as outrageously costumed revelers leaned
out of the car's many windows. It was as if the trolley
car, like New Orleans itself, was boiling over with excitement.

Annie drank it all in until the cab pulled up to an
elegant colonial mansion. As David paid the cabbie,
Annie marveled at the magnificent gardens surrounding
the home, at its elaborate wrought-iron fence and railings, sensing the majesty of the old house. And, like
Annie herself, tonight the place was coming alive. Her
thoughts drifted briefly to Ellis, wondering if he was as
consumed by the magic of the night as she was. A slight
feeling of melancholy fell over her when she realized it
should have been the two of them enjoying Carnival
together. But, surprisingly, the thought did not lead to

those familiar stabbing pains of betrayal. The festive evening just wouldn't allow her to dwell for long on painful memories.

As she and David mounted the front stairs and moved across the porch, through the mansion's graceful columns, Annie realized this fine old place had a special quality. It had surely known days of grandeur, and days of pain and sorrow. It seemed to possess an understated strength that recognized the traumas of a checkered history and the passing of time. Sensing a comraderie with the elegant structure, Annie gained a heightened feeling of strength and tranquility. Perhaps she, too, could withstand the passing of time and still stand strong.

A servant in colonial costume, complete with powered wig and knee breeches, ushered the couple into a magnificent ballroom. Annie smiled in delight. If the outside of the beautiful mansion was elegantly subdued, the party inside was something else. As David handed their wraps to another servant, Annie stared at the throng of gaily costumed guests dancing to a brassy band, laughing, drinking, and obviously enjoying themselves.

"Quite a bash, isn't it?" David smiled as he rejoined her.

Annie had to agree. And so the two of them dove into the fun. At first, Annie danced with David, but it wasn't long before she'd drawn the interest of several dashingly costumed men who begged her to dance with them. And Annie, thoroughly enjoying the flattery, abandoned herself to the moment, matching their best dance moves, giving in to the spontaniety of the evening. There was no magic carpet beneath Annie's sandaled feet, but, nevertheless, she felt as if she were floating as New Orleans and its powerful Mardi Gras atmosphere wove its spell on her.

As the night wore on, David and Annie strolled from

one elegant mansion to the next, and, for Annie, it was like a fresh awakening each place they went. Every party had its own exotic flavor. And David's circle of friends seemed to include just about all of the city's aristocracy and powerful businessmen. As David had predicted, the sensual attraction of Annie's costume did not go unnoticed. Many heads turned in her direction, and she noted them with building confidence. As she clocked the many appreciative male eyes scrutinizing her from behind their masks, she could barely suppress a giggle at the thought of how a sexy costume could alter her whole identity.

As she danced with an old friend of David's, she reacted to a joke, tossing her head back and laughing freely. She was beginning to feel as good as she looked. The few drinks she'd had and the subdued modern waltz her partner was guiding her through made her feel like she was floating. They waltzed smoothly across a highly polished, magnificent marble floor. He seemed a charming, easygoing fellow, and Annie, now succumbing to the demands of the long evening, rested her head easily against his shoulder. She was sure this wouldn't be taken as an enticing move. Annie was simply at ease.

She peered through lazy eyes in a half-closed assessment of her beautiful surroundings. She loved seeing her brightly painted toes moving across the creamy white marble. Glancing upward, she marveled at the expansive crystal chandelier overhead, which sent rainbow patterns across the huge room. She gazed idly over the other dancers, wondering if they shared her feelings of serenity. An elderly pair of frogs danced cheek to cheek with their eyes closed, obviously content, and Annie sighed. As her partner spun her around, she saw the back of a tall cavalier dancing with a Marie Antoinette who appeared to have stepped directly out of the French Revolution. The cavalier, in a blousy white silk shirt and crimson sash, complete with sword, cut a dashing figure. As her partner moved her around again, Annie lifted her head from his shoulder, and, through the tunnels created by passing dancers, saw the elegant figure guiding his partner across the floor in graceful rhythm.

Black, slick tights clung to his long, gracefully muscled legs, and Annie continued to stare, noting something familiar as the man maneuvered across the floor, chatting amusingly to his partner. She felt a gnawing sensation begin in the pit of her stomach as she watched the stranger gripping his partner's waist, strong arms outlined beneath his ruffled shirt. Then the couple spun around. Annie saw that he wore a small black domino mask. She stared in dismay at the hint of slate eyes behind the mask, confirming her fears. There could be no mistaking that graceful frame dancing across the floor, and Annie felt her knees weaken. Even masked and costumed, Annie knew it was Ellis. She felt her heart begin to pound wildly beneath her thin blouse, and fought the urge to bolt from the dance floor.

Her view was temporarily blocked by the scores of costumed couples all around her. Then, as a cowboy and cowgirl moved past her, she saw him again. And now, she realized, Marie Antoinette was Camille Du Maurier! Annie fought the bile that rose in her throat and tried to compose herself enough to ask her partner to end the dance. But before the request could reach her lips, the cavalier turned his head, and those gray eyes fixed themselves directly on Annie. It was as if Ellis's eyes were sending darts with unerring accuracy, striking her own wide hazel stare, holding her in a grip she was unable to break.

Suddenly, Ellis stopped dancing and broke away from Camille, squaring his shoulders in Annie's direction. His mouth seemed to part in a smile of recognition. Even though their faces were partially hidden behind their respective mask and veil, Annie was sure that Ellis's piercing eyes had uncovered her identity as surely as she had discovered his. Camille looked at Ellis, puzzled by the interruption of their dance . . . and Annie tried to look away. But she couldn't take her eyes off him as he stood, with his hands on his hips, grinning like a Barbary pirate who's just sighted bountiful plunder.

Annie resolutely turned her head away, placing it back on her partner's shoulder. By now, David's friend had sensed that something was wrong, but before he could ask Annie what was troubling her, Ellis strode up and tapped the man on the shoulder. The band struck up another number, and before she could protest, Ellis had her in his arms and was guiding her across the floor, never taking his eyes from hers.

Annie didn't need a mirror to know that her cheeks were flushing red. She simply hoped that the little veil would hide some of her distress. Although she wanted nothing more than to tear herself away, she found she could barely stand. Being in his arms once again was like being in the grip of a paralyzing spell from which there was no escape. High above her, the chandelier seemed to spin and sway, and a flash of bright prisms whirled dizzyingly around her. Ellis's sudden appearance seemed to make time stop. These were no imaginary arms which held her! This tall costumed figure was no apparition. His arm tightened around her waist, drawing her closer, sending a searing shiver through her. Annie summoned all her willpower to respond to his bold move.

"Ellis, I . . . I don't feel like dancing right now. Please excuse me." She turned her head, about to step away, but Ellis merely pulled her more tightly to him. The warmth of his powerful body radiated out, spreading through Annie, kindling a familiar and unwelcome flame of desire.

His husky reply, murmured into her ear, did nothing

to diminish the effect. "You don't really expect me to let you walk away that easily, do you, Annie?" he said sardonically.

Annie kept her head turned away, unable to face him. "Please, Ellis," she managed, hating herself for pleading with him, "let me go."

"I think not." Taking her chin delicately with the thumb and forefinger of his left hand, Ellis turned her head, forcing Annie to look directly into his eyes. "Here I am, dancing with the most beautiful creature at this ball, and I intend to take advantage of my good fortune." Annie felt naked beneath his knowing stare, saw that his eyes were sparkling as they crinkled around the edges of the domino mask.

She jerked her head from his grasp and scanned the room. Where was David now that she needed him? Annie spotted him by the buffet table, chatting amiably to a few people, totally unaware of her predicament. Annie was on her own. Trying to keep her voice from cracking, she turned back to Ellis and replied, "I don't care *what* you intend. You will never take advantage of me again. So if you will kindly let go of me, I'd like to get back to enjoying the party."

Ellis's smile vanished, but his grip around her waist didn't loosen. "I don't know how you can say that, Annie. When I saw you here, I felt a sense of relief. I can't believe that you don't share those feelings."

Annie didn't want to discuss feelings—hers or Ellis's. His disturbing presence was wearing down the confidence she'd so carefully nurtured. She had to break away from his spell while she could.

But Ellis hadn't finished yet. "And anyway, this is *my* dance," he said firmly, "and I intend to finish it."

"This dance is over, as far as I'm concerned," Annie replied. "Besides, hadn't you better get back to your *date?"* She spat out this reference to Camille as though it had a bad taste.

"It's you I'm worried about, Annie, and my date, as you put it, can manage on her own for a while."

Annie glanced around the room, and sure enough, Camille was nowhere in sight. Ellis's full attention was directed solely on her. Annie felt as if the room was closing in on her. The orchestra played out the last few bars of the musical number, and, as dancers began to separate and wander off, she saw her opportunity to get away.

"You've had your dance . . ." and unable to say good-bye, she wrenched herself from his grasp. As she moved away, she fought the urge to look back, and clenching her fists, Annie wove her way across the crowded floor. An open pair of French doors led to a patio, and Annie darted through them. Her sandaled feet barely made a sound as she fled across the stone patio and into the expansive gardens which fanned out from the rear of the mansion.

A welcome darkness shrouded her as she moved deeper and deeper into the wooded splendor of the gardens. The full moon overhead, peeking out from behind its own mask of wispy clouds, lit her path as she moved in and out of the shadows, away from the party atmosphere of the house, into the peaceful tranquility of the flowers and manicured shrubs. The late-night air breezed cool and gentle across Annie's flushed cheeks as she slowed down to catch her breath. Her heart still pounded rapidly but the serenity of the garden provided a soothing balm and she halted beneath a moonlit magnolia tree, rising above a carpet of its own white flowers.

How could fate be so cruel and bring him back into her life this fast, she pondered. She had tried her best not to be affected by his presence, and yet, just moments ago, Ellis had managed to send her mind reeling. Annie's logic and her stoic determination had suddenly melted as Ellis's piercing eyes stared through her emotional armor as easily as they·saw through the flimsy fabric of her costume.

She resumed her walk, as if each step deeper into the garden could take her further from his haunting presence. Spotting a charming white gazebo, Annie strolled toward it, mounting the steps to the little summerhouse as the breeze picked up, and the heady scent of night-blooming jasmine filled the air with its perfume. Annie inhaled deeply, hoping the flowery aroma would chase the problems out of her head. With a pleasurable sigh, she leaned against the railing, brushing a stray lock of auburn hair away from her warm forehead. As Annie stared up at the moon, a voice broke her solitude.

"It's a little like magic, don't you think?" Annie turned, dismayed, to see Ellis standing at the foot of the stairs, gazing past her to the moon overhead.

Damn him, she thought. How dare he follow her and intrude on her privacy this way? She silently retreated up the last step, not bothering to answer him. As if on cue, Ellis took another step himself, so that he was able to lean over lazily on one knee. Breaking into a smile, he paid no attention to Annie's silence.

"That's quite a costume, Annie. If I didn't know better, I'd swear a genie passing through had left me with a spare wish on his way out of town."

Annie's first impulse was to move further into the shadows of the little gazebo, but it was no use. The structure was tiny, and, with the colluding moon poking its face out to illuminate her distress, there was nowhere to hide.

"You enjoy slinking around in the dark, frightening helpless ladies, do you?" she asked sarcastically, a defiant hand on her hip.

Ellis stood up straight and whipped off his mask. "You misinterpret my actions. I assure you, my intentions are solely honorable . . . or, at least, they were until I saw that costume of yours in the moonlight." Annie felt herself shiver as Ellis continued, a smile playing on his lips, "And you're a far cry from a helpless lady."

"What do you want, Ellis? Why did you follow me?" Annie demanded impatiently, tired of these verbal games.

"I want you, Annie. You know that." His expression was hard. "It may be easy for you to turn off your feelings whenever it's convenient, but I can't do that. When I commit myself to someone or something, I can't simply drop them flat."

"What do you know about commitment?" Annie retorted. "If what you've given me is your standard prescription, *Doctor,* then I'm glad I'm no longer one of your patients."

Ellis's quick move brought him up and into the gazebo. With one powerful hand, he grabbed her by the wrist, and with the other, he ripped off her little veil. "Let's quit playing games, shall we?"

It was not a question, it was a command. And Annie felt herself melting beneath the smoldering desire that seemed to exude from his every pore. But she pulled back, reflexively, crying out, "Ellis, my arm! You're hurting me."

He eased his grip momentarily, simply staring, as the glinting moonlight, radiating through the latticework above, illuminated them and bright diamonds seemed to halo around Annie. Then he reached out a demanding arm and took her by the waist, drawing her close.

"I love you, Annie. Whatever else you may think— or suspect—you must believe that."

Annie's mind reeled. It was what she had wanted to hear for so long! But how could she believe him? How could she trust this man who seemingly toyed with her emotions, who had never offered any explanation of his behavior? She *wanted* to believe it, wanted it more than anything in the world. And now, with Ellis's warm breath so close to her ear, with his free arm reaching to cradle the back of her head, tilting her mouth upwards, Annie found herself responding.

She gave way to her emotions, and, with a soft sigh of pleasure, threw her arms around his neck, as if to take his kiss and draw it into her very soul. The breeze picked up once again, causing Annie's light costume to billow around her, bringing the magical fragrance of the night-blooming jasmine with it. She swayed, wrapped in his embrace, welcoming his gently probing tongue, his tender rediscovery. Ellis's own masculine scent, combined with the heady jasmine was a powerful elixir drowning Annie's senses. She felt herself consumed, caught up in the fiery bliss which recalled her most passionate memories. It seemed as if everything that had happened to destroy what had been between them had never occurred. It was simply swept away in this blaze.

It was only moments since their embrace had begun, but to Annie, it seemed an eternity. She felt Ellis relax his hold on her, and she opened her eyes in surprise. He drew his head back gently, breaking the moment, and Annie caught her breath. She stared deeply into his somber eyes, searching, hoping to find the truth there. Bathed in the glow of the moonlight it was as if she and Ellis and the gazebo itself were of another time and place. She raised herself on tiptoes, eagerly offering her mouth to him again, but, oddly, Ellis withdrew, moving back to arm's length and holding her there.

"Wait, Annie."

"Ellis, what's wrong?" Annie asked, confused by his behavior.

"Nothing, Annie . . . I just don't want this to happen so fast that you'll wonder about me later. You may think this strange, but I need your love and your trust as much as I want your body."

His frank proclamation startled her. She had let down her defenses during those brief moments of passion, but still hadn't resolved the nagging questions that plagued her.

"I don't know about trust right now, Ellis, but I can't deny what I feel for you anymore. Surely you must know how much I . . . I, how much I'm in love with you." There, she had said it.

"I just told you, Annie," Ellis said patiently, "I must have your trust, too. I can't open my feelings to you only to have you cut me off when there are things you don't understand, or the moment you feel any doubts."

Annie couldn't believe what she was hearing. He spoke of trust, of her ability to hurt him. Didn't he realize that it was his own evasiveness which had ripped them apart?

Annie swallowed hard to prevent the lump she felt rising in her throat. "It was you who lied, Ellis, not me. How can you expect me to put my trust in someone who does that to the woman he claims to love?"

"Please, Annie, let's not spoil this evening by trading foolish accusations." Ellis's words were measured.

Annie stepped back and looked hard at him. Why was he persisting in his evasions, she wondered. What did he have to hide from her? Something inside her knew she could no longer avoid the issue. "It appears," she said, choosing her words carefully, "that you have something you're hiding from me. If not, why don't you explain what is going on between you and Camille Du Maurier?" she prodded, hating herself for ruining the moment, but needing to know the truth.

"Annie, you don't know what you're talking about. It's you I care about, not Camille." Taking her hand, he led Annie to a small bench in the gazebo. "I've thought of little else since you stormed away from the restaurant that evening. I was afraid I'd never see you again, and now, being with you, holding you in my arms...Annie, believe me, you're the best thing that's ever happened to me, and I don't want to lose you again."

However much she wanted to believe him, things still didn't seem right, and the doubt that had earlier consumed her, threatened to do so again. The thought of testing Ellis was abhorrent but Annie knew she couldn't afford any more devastation.

"Ellis, take me away from here, right now," she said impulsively. "Let's just escape into the night and leave all this behind us." She stood up, taking his hand, as if to lead him away. But Ellis's hesitation, and then the withdrawal of his hand from hers sent a deep churning fear through Annie.

"Oh, there you are, Ellis! I couldn't imagine where you'd run off to." The musical voice pierced the night and Annie turned with a start to see Marie Antoinette climbing into the gazebo.

"Ellis, something's come up and..." she paused, noticing Annie. "Oh, hello," Camille said, scrutinizing Annie's costume, "you're Anne Carroll, aren't you?"

Annie, at a loss for polite words, merely nodded.

"Well, I'm sorry, but I'm afraid I'll have to ask if you'll be so kind as to excuse us....Ellis and I have some important private matters to discuss."

Camille's voice was calm and businesslike but the implications of her words seared Annie like a hot poker. She looked enquiringly at Ellis for his reaction to this request.

Ellis's mouth was set in a grim line as he nodded.

"Annie, we need a few minutes, okay?"

"Of course, Ellis. Good bye." Annie managed the few polite words and quickly left the gazebo. In the background, she could still hear Camille's voice addressing Ellis, and, wanting to block the whole thing from her mind, she picked up her pace and headed for the house.

She stepped through the French doors to where the party was still in full swing. Looking over the heads of the many dancers, Annie spotted David, in the arms of a female vampire. As Annie weaved her way through the moving couples, David spotted her, whispered something to his partner and then walked over to Annie.

David breathed a sigh of relief as he grasped Annie around the waist and began guiding her to the light beat of the jazz combo playing in the background. "Boy, you showed up just in the nick of time. That gal may look like a vampire on the outside but inside she's a cobra. Advertising manager for our friendly rivals at WKBY. Talked my ear off trying to find out our new logo." David was cheery and oblivious to Annie's troubled state of affairs, until he noted her distant gaze. "Say, you okay?"

Annie looked up at David with a start. "Uh, sure, David. . . . It's just that I'm not feeling all that great at the moment. I think I'd feel better if I went home."

"That's too bad, Annie," David said with a note of concern in his voice. "I'll grab us a cab. I think I'm about partied out by now anyway."

"No, David, it's still early. Don't let me spoil your evening. I'll be fine, really, I'll just. . ." Annie let the words fade as David responded to a tap on his shoulder and both he and Annie looked up to see Ellis standing there with every intention of stepping in to take Annie.

"Hello, David, nice costume. Be a sport and let me have Annie for the next one." Before either David or Annie could protest Ellis took Annie in his arms and proceeded to glide across the floor to the music, totally unaffected by the daggers Annie shot from her narrowed hazel eyes.

"Ellis, I'm not up for any more of your schoolboy moves," Annie spat venomously. "Let me go, will you?" She struggled within his grip.

"Not so fast, Annie," Ellis replied, staring down at her, holding her waist close against his swaying body. "I can't let you go off thinking something that's not true."

"I don't know what to think anymore," she said softly, while unconsciously matching his movements across the marble floor. "All I know is that every time you ask me to trust you, I see you sneaking around with that . . . with Camille."

"She means nothing to me, I've told you that, Annie," Ellis's voice sounded sincere but Annie remained unconvinced.

"Yes, you have told me that, haven't you?" She continued, "It seems like you're always telling me that. Don't you think it's time for a new line, *Doctor?* Your old one's a bit worn." The music was building to a crescendo and, as the number drew to a close, Annie decided she'd had enough dancing. At the edge of the dance floor, she saw Camille, watching them attentively.

"Annie, don't be so quick to judge. You're making a terrible mistake about me. It's not fair, to me or to yourself." Ellis's brow furrowed in confusion, as if he labored for just the right words.

But Annie was in no mood to argue with him anymore. With her lips twisting into a sneer, she broke from his grasp and, indicating Camille with a nod of her head, offered, "I hope you enjoyed your dance, Ellis, I doubt we'll be doing it again. Besides, your *friend* is waiting for you. Try your lines on her, why don't you, I'm tired of them. It looks to me like you're playing both ends against the middle and I, for one, don't like being used this way." Fighting for control in her voice, Annie lifted her head, stared directly into Ellis's eyes and pronounced, "If you'll excuse me..." And before Ellis could reply, Annie moved away through the throng of dispersing dancers, leaving Ellis standing alone, staring after her.

CHAPTER
Nine

WRAPPING HER SHAWL tightly around her shoulders, Annie stepped off the mansion's towering porch and proceeded across the lawn, toward the street, searching for a cab.

A mixture of anger and pain coursed through her, jumbling her thoughts to the point that she didn't even realize she'd stepped into the wide strip of tulips which bordered the wrought-iron fence surrounding the mansion. The wet squish of her thoroughly ruined sandles signaled her blunder.

She cursed inwardly and stepped through the wide gateway onto Saint Charles Avenue. The balmy night air was still filled with the sounds of party celebrants, and all around her, costumed figures moved in and out of the many houses that lined the elegant street.

Damn! Where was a taxi when she needed it most, Annie breathed in frustration as she scanned the street. The clip-clop of horses hooves eventually reached her ears, growing louder, until Annie saw a horse-drawn hansom cab approach. It stopped near her and an elderly couple, dressed in ballroom finery, emerged from the high-wheeled carriage. The driver tipped his top hat to the elderly gentleman and seeing Annie, he gestured toward the waiting carriage. Why not? she thought.

Annie settled into the tufted leather seat and the cab started with a springy lurch. It quickly picked up speed and the two horses, moving easily into a medium gait, beat a light merry rhythm with their hooves on the paved street. The gentle bouncy motion of the vehicle was a welcome relief after her run in with Ellis at the party and it almost made her forget her dance-weary feet and wet sandals.

All around her the festivities of Mardi Gras continued in full swing. She tried not to think of Ellis and his apparent affair with Camille by drinking in the gentle breeze that drifted past her as the coach continued intrepidly through the raucous crowds that filled the streets.

A streetcar, filled with costumed figures, gawking bizarrely through the windows, passed by Annie in the opposite direction. A makeshift float, carrying brightly costumed African dancers, led a parade of bands, floats, and tourists across her path. Music seemed to pour from every corner of New Orleans.

Finally, the driver turned onto a quiet street. Annie welcomed the lack of noise and eased back into her seat. In the distance, the gentle, cheery music of a steel band chimed and faded as Annie relaxed and the coach continued on its jaunty voyage.

"M'am, we're here...ma'am?" The driver's gentle voice brought Annie back to the present and she looked up to see the smiling driver as he held open the little carriage door for her. Annie paid the man and, after tipping his hat to her, he issued a friendly command to the horses and was off in search of another fare.

Annie turned toward her apartment door when out of the corner of her eye she spotted a dark blue Jaguar parked at the curb. The car's familiarity was confirmed as she turned again toward the entrance to her building and there, sitting on the stoop, was none other than Ellis, still in costume, waiting for her.

"I don't believe it," Annie said incredulously. "I thought I'd made it clear, Ellis, I don't want you following me around wherever I go." She brushed past him into her building without a backward glance, but the rustle of Ellis's costume told her he was quick at her heels.

As Annie reached her door and put her key to the lock, Ellis spoke, his breath warm on the back of her neck.

"Annie, wait! I only came because there's something I think you should know."

"I think I've heard enough," she replied as she opened the door and started to close it behind her.

Ellis quickly placed his hand against it, holding the door open. "Don't be pigheaded, Annie. I've got something to tell you, something very important and you must hear me out, okay? Afterwards, if you still feel the same, then throw me out." Ellis's tone was calm, not pleading and the look in his eyes demanded an answer.

Annie searched Ellis's face trying to gauge his sincerity, finally realizing that, whatever he had to say to her, was evidently important enough for him to put himself on the line, risking her disapproval for perhaps the last time. She tore her gaze from the intensity of his eyes and stood back from the door. Ellis followed her inside and closed the door behind him.

Standing in the center of her living room, Annie turned back toward him, arms across her chest. "Okay, I'm listening."

It was obvious he didn't care for her blunt, curt manner, but Ellis began nevertheless. "First of all, Annie, you must promise that everything I tell you will remain in this room. I can't have you blurting it out over the television or anywhere else. Understand?" Ellis's firm demand came as a surprise but now Anne's curiosity outweighed her vexation with him.

Annie walked over to a dark wood cabinet, grabbed a couple of brandy snifters and a bottle of French cognac and poured two stiff shots. Handing one to Ellis, she replied, "You have my word, Ellis."

He took a sip and then, wiping an errant drop of liquor from the corner of his mouth, he began. "After you left the party, it was clear my asking you to give me time to explain would never work. I made a phone call to Senator Jaynes and asked, no I almost begged him to let me tell you what we've been doing. I promised you'd keep his secret. . . . My professional reputation is on the line, Annie, do you understand?"

She didn't like his sudden overbearing manner, as if he were a ramrod schoolteacher, talking down to an upstart pupil. She took a sip of her drink while staring back at Ellis over the rim of her glass. He took a step toward her and Annie retreated to her couch, avoiding the commanding presence of Ellis's tall, sleek body. His penetrating stare was matched by her own intense scrutiny. "What is it?" she demanded.

His tone softened. "Annie, you must understand that from the onset, I had no choice about keeping this particular secret from you. The night I canceled dinner with you—the night you came into La Vie en Rose with David—I'd gotten a call from Camille Du Maurier that afternoon. She told me that she had to speak with me, that her father was gravely ill. He'd just flown back from the Mayo clinic, where he'd been told he had less than a twenty percent chance of living out the year. The problem was his heart."

Annie nodded, understanding the gravity of the problem.

"Well, Camille is an old friend, Annie." At her arched eyebrow, Ellis smiled tightly. "Okay, we were engaged but that was ages ago—my God, Annie, we were kids.

Both of us realized that we wanted very different things out of life and that was that. But we've always been friends. Anyway, Camille wanted me to see the Senator—make my own examination and see if there was anything I could think of that the other doctors might have overlooked. After all, it is my area."

Ellis paused and sipped his drink. Then he looked seriously at Annie. "There was no way I could turn her down. There was no way I would have *wanted* to turn her down. I've known that family since I was born and the Senator was a close friend of my parents. If there was anything I could possibly do, I had to do it." He smiled ruefully at Annie. "It just happened to be the worst night anyone could have picked to need me—the night I had so carefully planned to tell you how damned much I love you—how I want to spend the rest of my life with you. Oh, Annie, what a mess!"

Annie caught her breath. As much as she had known that she loved this man she hadn't known how much it would mean to hear those words from him. Oh, God, what a fool she'd been, to be so suspicious, to cause all these problems, to tear them apart when they might have been sharing so much precious time together.

"Anyway," Ellis continued, "the Senator couldn't see me until later that night so I took Camille out to cheer her up, comfort her if I could. Later, after I examined him, I realized that there was an incredibly tough choice to make. I'd been researching a new heart surgery technique, one which could stop the deterioration of certain valves—precisely the problem that plagued the senator. But the surgery was still in the early, experimental stages. I hadn't wanted to use it on a human so soon but Camille and her father begged me to try my technique on him. After all, they said, if he was going to die within a year anyway, why not try it? At least, no matter what the outcome, he'd have helped advance a new surgical technique which might eventually save thousands of lives."

"Oh, Ellis, why didn't you tell me?" she asked. "I thought...I thought you..." Her voice trailed off and she simply stared at him, hazel eyes wide with love and compassion.

"I know what you must've thought, Annie," he said gently, "but I was sworn to secrecy. No matter what I decided—whether to risk surgery or not—this was no time for anyone to know about the Senator's illness. He's up for reelection and he's been involved in some very delicate international negotiations. If any of this leaked out, his political enemies would have a field day."

"Is...is he all right now?" Annie asked.

"Yes. He should recover fully. Do you understand now why I couldn't tell you any of this, Annie?"

"Yes, darling, of course I do." Annie spoke softly.

"Good," Ellis nodded grimly. "There were times when I thought you never would. You've the devil's own knack for turning up just when it looks like I'm doing something I shouldn't be. And you're not the most forgiving woman I've ever met, either."

"I know," Annie replied apologetically. "I just didn't believe that it was possible to feel so much for someone and to give myself so completely. When it happened and then you seemed to be, well, lying, I guess I went a little crazy. I...I felt so used, so betrayed."

"Used? My God, Annie, how could you have felt like that? Everything between us—right up until then—was going perfectly. At least," Ellis reflected soberly, "I thought it was perfect."

Annie struggled to get the words out correctly. "It was. It seemed perfect to me too, Ellis."

"There was nothing I could do to make you understand without betraying a confidence. I wanted you to just take it at face value . . . to believe me completely. Instead, it was like an impenetrable wall had dropped between us."

"I guess I've still got a lot of defenses to get rid of," Annie said slowly. "But Ellis, you must believe me, I've never felt like this before. It scared me. It was like having paradise opened up to my vision and then, suddenly, bam! The gates were closed and I was out in the cold, confused, hurt, and angry." She gazed up into his intense gray eyes. They seemed to be reading right into her soul. "Can you understand that?"

"I think I can," he replied. "But you must understand that your penchant for believing the worst put me in a tough position. I shouldn't have had to go back to the Senator on this. Sometimes I wonder if you'll ever be willing to give me the benefit of the doubt. Annie, you have to start believing in someone, sometime. And that someone should be me. I love you far too much to want to hurt you." Ellis cupped her face gently in his hands. "When I told you out in the gazebo that I was in love with you, it was the only way I could think of to buy some time—to try to keep you from closing me out of your life altogether. It was bad timing, I admit, and I know it must have seemed ridiculous, considering the circumstances. But it was the truth—I won't ever lie to you darling. Do you believe me?"

"Oh, yes," Annie breathed, her heart pounding. If it took the most supreme, conscientious effort of all time, she'd never allow herself to be swept with doubt and fear by the things that Ellis did or said.

Ellis held her tightly and queried, "No more misunderstandings?" He stroked her hair.

"No, no more misunderstandings," Annie replied, turning her mouth up to meet his for a breathless, fiery kiss.

They broke apart, content for the moment to enjoy the comfort and pleasure of simply being in each other's arms.

CHAPTER

Ten

"IT SEEMS LIKE forever since we were together."

"Only three, no four days," Annie murmured into Ellis's chest, running her lips lightly across the well-muscled chest.

He hugged her even more tightly to him. "What do you mean by 'only'?" he demanded teasingly. "Although I can't really complain." He tilted her chin up so her sleepy hazel eyes met his smoky gaze, "Since you show a certain propensity toward, shall we say, making up for lost time?"

Annie giggled. "I do hate wasted time," she assured him.

"It shows." Ellis grinned at her. "But I'm losing my strength. How does some breakfast sound?"

"Great," Annie replied lazily, stifling a yawn.

Ellis regarded her with mock severity. "What'll it take to get you out of bed?"

"I'll probably get lonely—or bored—after you leave," Annie said solemnly.

Ellis raised one thick, black eyebrow. "I'm not even going to touch that one," he said. "Except, does that 'after you've gone' bit mean that I'm supposed to make breakfast?"

"Well...I'll help," Annie conceded. "But I want to shower first, okay?"

"All right," Ellis agreed. "I'll see you in the kitchen—and don't be long!"

"Yes, sir!" Annie said, watching as, in one energetic movement, Ellis was out of bed and halfway across the big bedroom. He pulled on a charcoal terrycloth robe and disappeared into the hall.

Annie sighed and propelled herself reluctantly out of bed, too. She stretched and yawned as she padded naked into the large master bath and turned on the steaming shower. It was funny, she mused, how comfortable she was in Ellis's house. It was almost like home.

All week, ever since Ellis had explained things to her the night of Mardi Gras, both of their schedules had been too hectic and unpredictable to allow them any time together. They hadn't managed to see each other until Saturday night. But, Annie reflected, smiling as she stepped into the shower, Ellis had been right on the mark when he observed that she did her best to make up for lost time—as did he. She continued smiling as hot water streamed over her, remembering the intensity and passion of the previous night.

Maybe things could work out for them after all, she reflected. She loved Ellis; there could be no question about that, not any more. And, now that she knew what had really gone on during those terrible days after she'd seen him with Camille at La Vie en Rose, Annie was calmer than she had been before: he was someone she could trust, as well as someone she could love. Of course, Ellis hadn't really spoken about the future. At least, not yet. And Annie was resolved not to push anything.

She stepped out of the shower, drying herself briskly with a plush black bathsheet. All in good time, she told herself. But still, she thought, pulling on jeans and a soft blue sweater, they were so *good* together. In every way. What would it be like to be together all the time? Well, she amended her thoughts, making allowances for their unpredictable schedules, as much of the time as possible? Taking the stairs two at a time down to the bright kitchen, it felt like a wonderful idea.

"That was quick," Ellis commented, turning from the range, where he was watching a pan of bacon. "I thought I'd have to come upstairs and drag you down here."

"I told you I'd help," Annie protested. "I'll make the o.j.," she volunteered, turning toward the juicer.

Ellis smiled at her from across the room. "You look adorable this morning—all fresh and bright."

"I had a terrific night," Annie assured him, keeping a resolutely straight face. "It's amazing what a night like that can do for the complexion..."

"And the gleam in your eye," Ellis chimed in.

"Maybe it's something you should turn your attention to," Annie's mouth began to curve. "Speaking medically, of course... You know, a research project."

Ellis crossed the room swiftly, pulling her toward him with a firm grasp on her slender waist. "Mmm," he said, burying his face in her neck. His hands moved upward, lightly stroking her rib cage, delicately brushing her rounded breasts. "I'd love to keep this kind of research up... for a long, long time."

Annie's arms tightened automatically around his shoulders, and they swayed against the counter in a long, exploratory kiss, until Ellis pulled back.

"What's the matter?" Annie queried innocently. "Don't you like necking like a teenager? Too old for this kind of nonsense, Ellis?"

"The question is, do you or don't you want breakfast?" he countered sternly, brushing a lock of black hair off his forehead.

"Oh, I do," Annie assured him, turning back to the juicer. Then, she glanced over her shoulder and grinned impishly. *"I* wasn't the one who started..."

"Work!" Ellis commanded.

Later, as they relaxed over coffee and fresh strawberries drenched in heavy cream, Annie studied Ellis's angular handsome face. It was calm, peaceful. She wondered what it would be like to face the kind of life-and-death situations he did every day. Well, she reflected, he certainly played as hard as he worked.

"What are you looking so pensive about?" he asked.

"I was thinking about your work," Annie replied. "The stress involved, how you relax." She shrugged, smiling a bit. "And the quality of time—the time we spend together, specifically."

"Good?" Ellis's gaze was probing.

Annie nodded. "Very good," she said quietly. Then she checked her watch and gasped. "Oh, no," she wailed, "I've got to go—there's a story which needs work, and..."

"It's okay," Ellis said, "I understand."

"I thought you would." Annie pushed her chair back from the table. "Oh, Ellis, before I forget, Nancy gave me her tickets to the ballet on Tuesday night. She and Kevin have to work. Want to go?"

Ellis glanced down at the table, then back up at Annie. "Tuesday? No, no I don't think so, Annie."

"Why not?" she asked, knowing Ellis liked the ballet.

"It's just, well, I'm pretty sure I'm going to be tied up that night," he replied evasively.

"Oh," Annie said blankly, feeling let down. Then, reminding herself that she trusted Ellis, she brightened her voice. "Okay, no big deal," she said, dismissing the subject.

She retrieved her purse and shoes, then kissed him lightly. "Talk to you later," she said, keeping her voice cheerful.

Ellis seemed preoccupied as she left, she thought. But

she firmly banished all negative thoughts from her mind. If Ellis chose to be reticent, he was doing so for a good reason. After the events of only a week ago, she simply had to believe that.

"Annie! Hi, babe, what's up?" Jackson Cahill slid onto his stool behind the deskfront which served as the set for their newscast. "You look great."

"Thanks, Jackson," Annie smiled. Ever since her Craig Bolding story had gone national, Jackson had accorded her more stature as a fellow reporter. His familiarity and friendliness had come as an added bonus, a sort of reward, letting her know she'd finally arrived as a newscaster.

"Good weekend?" he asked casually, readjusting one perfect strand of silver hair.

"Terrific," Annie replied.

"It shows." Jackson smiled at her.

"Really," David echoed from behind them.

Annie swiveled on her stool to say hello to the news director, who had an odd, reserved look on his easygoing face.

"What's up, David?" Annie asked.

"I just saw the UPI bulletin about Ellis. Honestly, Annie, I would really have preferred to hear that kind of news from you." David's expression was quizzical and slightly upset.

"I don't know what you're talking about," Annie said, bewildered by David's tone and words.

David stared at her, disbelief crossing his handsome features. "The Johns Hopkins position," he said. "Don't tell me that you didn't know . . ."

"Twenty seconds," the assistant director called out, and David vanished abruptly from the range of the camera's eye.

"David, what . . ." Annie started to call out, but closed

her mouth as the red light came on.

"Good evening, this is Jackson Cahill."

"And Anne Carroll," she said automatically, then pushed all thoughts of David's words out of her head: she had a job to do. But the second she was off camera, Annie swung off her stool and jogged over to where David stood, clipboard in hand.

"David, about what you said before the broadcast," she began.

David fixed a serious blue gaze on her. "Annie, if you really don't know, I apologize for leaping to conclusions . . . but I think you'd better go take a look at the UPI tickertape."

"All right," Annie agreed wonderingly. It was obvious that David had no intention of being the bearer of bad news in this particular case!

As she crossed the station floor to the spot where the UPI and AP machines stood, spitting out up-to-the-minute information, she passed Monica, who was hurrying from the machines back toward her desk.

"Are you really moving to Baltimore?" she asked Annie, concern in her large brown eyes.

"Not that I was aware of," Annie replied grimly. What the hell was going on here? she wondered.

As she stood over the machine, scanning the long, slender tape which cascaded into curls on the floor of the newsroom, she finally located the news item which everyone—except herself—seemed to know already. It was an announcement from the head of the Johns Hopkins Medical Center in Baltimore: Ellis Greystone, prominent and innovative cardiologist, best known for his recent life-prolonging surgery on Senator John Jaynes of Louisiana, had been named the new head of Cardiology at Johns Hopkins. Annie's wide, startled eyes raced over the tape: Greystone's background included, etc., etc. . . .

As she finished the news flash, she shook her head in disbelief. How could this be happening? How long had Ellis known about this? She remembered with perfect clarity, of course, his trip to Baltimore. The night he'd returned home had been the first time they'd made love. But, since then, there had been little mention of Johns Hopkins. And certainly nothing had been said about relocating to Baltimore! If this was true—and it was hard to argue with a planned statement which came over the UPI tape—then just how long had Ellis been aware that he was moving away from New Orleans—and away from her? There it was, in black and white, that the "well-known" surgeon had accepted the position; not just been offered it, but had *accepted* it.

Annie's wide hazel eyes narrowed in anger and dismay, and she turned abruptly away from the machine, her head awhirl with confusion. As she strode back toward her glassed-in cubicle, she was grimly determined to get this particular issue cleared up, post haste!

Ellis had said he loved her. If that was true, how could he have done something like this? Could he have been stringing her along all this time, after all. Could it all have been just an act? Had he really planned to accept this position and move away, without even telling her? Leave her behind, a discarded lover? As the thoughts flew through her mind, Annie grew more and more furious.

Slamming the door behind her, she flung herself into her chair, and, without hesitating, dialed the hospital. But, she wasn't going to get any satisfaction from the call, she realized, as the head nurse informed her that Ellis was tied up indefinitely in emergency surgery. Fuming, Annie left her name, making sure that the woman put an "urgent" on the message. As she sat glaring at the silent phone, her office door opened.

"Hey, Carroll," David's tone was apologetic, "I'm

sorry, honest, I just assumed . . ."

Annie's words were icy. "I love the way everyone simply *assumes* things! she said sarcastically. "I wonder what Ellis was assuming when he accepted this position."

"Well," David countered mildly, "he's probably assuming that you'll go with him. At least," he added, "that's what I thought when I saw the bulletin."

Annie gazed up, surprised. That possibility hadn't even occurred to her. But now that David had suggested it—well, so what? Even if that *were* the case, it was almost as bad as Ellis planning to leave the city without her. He had absolutely no right to make any plans for their future without consulting her. And, she thought, temper rising by the moment, if that was what he had done, he was even more of a thoughtless chauvinist than she'd ever been able to imagine! Pick up and leave New Orleans, her career, her friends—without so much as being consulted? He had to be mad! What a choice, she reflected mirthlessly—either he was completely underhanded or just plain thoughtlessly crazy.

"Annie, are you okay?" David's worried voice snapped her back to the present.

She stared at him, her eyes sparking with anger. "Fine," she replied through gritted teeth. "Just fine! But David, I'd like to be alone, if you don't mind."

"No problem," he said politely, then shut the door behind him.

Annie sagged in her chair, relieved to be alone. There was nothing she wanted right now other than to be left to her own devices—and to wait for Ellis's call.

But the phone didn't ring. The time crawled by while Annie fumed, until it was time for the eleven o'clock broadcast. Annie went grimly through her part, hiding her emotional turmoil behind her professional mask. The people on the WJNO staff who'd heard the news had the good sense to stay away from the subject, warned off by the angry spark in her eyes.

At the conclusion of the late-night edition, Annie stopped to check if there were any messages. There was still no call from Ellis. On the drive home, Annie calmed herself down slightly; there was no sense in getting this upset over something she didn't have all the information about, she told herself. And she wouldn't have that until she'd spoken to Ellis himself.

She undressed and made herself a cup of herb tea, then climbed into bed. Just as she was dropping off to sleep, the phone rang.

Ellis, she realized, sounded exhausted. "Hi, darling," he said. "What's the matter? The message said urgent."

Annie felt a pang of guilt. He'd just emerged from a lengthy, complicated surgery: this was hardly the time to get into a personal confrontation.

"Ellis," she said, keeping her voice calm, "I'm sorry. It's nothing that can't wait till tomorrow—you sound absolutely beat."

"I am," he agreed, "but what's so . . ."

"No," Annie interrupted firmly. She wanted him wide awake when she brought up this particular subject. "It will keep, but I do need to talk to you. What are you doing in the morning?"

"Nothing scheduled," he replied, unsuccessfully stifling a yawn. "Want to meet me on the *Aurora?* We can have some coffee, take her out for a spin."

"That's fine," Annie said. "Ten-ish okay?"

"Yes," Ellis said wearily. "See you then, darling."

"Right," Annie said grimly. "Sleep well."

Annie spent a restless night, and woke still tired and anxious. The morning was overcast and strangely still. As she pulled her little car into the slip at the marina, a light rain began to fall. Annie could see Ellis's Jag already parked, and, trying to quell her anxiety, she jogged down the dock.

"Permission to board?" she called out, and Ellis appeared, reaching out a firm grasp to help her aboard.

"Hi," he said, kissing her lightly on the lips. Then he looked up. "Rain," he remarked.

"Yes . . . maybe we should just stay here," Annie suggested.

Ellis shrugged. "All right—the less exertion for me, the better, this morning. God, what a night! Come on below and help me get some coffee."

Annie followed obediently, thinking she must be doing a good job of acting. Ellis hadn't seemed to notice her sober demeanor or the dangerous glint in her eyes. They brought their coffee and rolls up on the deck, and settled into comfortable chaises, protected from the rain by a gaily striped awning. But, perhaps Ellis had noticed more than she thought, because as soon as they were settled, he turned serious gray eyes on her.

"Now, what's all this about?" he asked. "You aren't the type to leave an urgent message unless there's something wrong."

Annie took a deliberate sip of the steaming coffee, then met Ellis's eyes resolutely. "Ellis," she began, "I saw the UPI bulletin last night. There was an announcement that you'd been offered—and had accepted—the position at John Hopkins. Is it true?" She looked earnestly at him, hoping against hope that he'd say it was all a mistake.

Ellis's eyes darkened. "Dammit!" he exclaimed. "Can't anything be a surprise?"

"A surprise?" Annie echoed blankly, taken aback by his reaction to her question. He just seemed annoyed—

not shocked, not guilty—certainly not sorry. "What do you mean by that?" she asked uncertainly.

"Oh, Annie, that's why I told you I couldn't go to the ballet with you tonight—I have to fly up there and sign the papers, attend a conference tomorrow. You know, business. I wasn't going to tell you until it was all official." He still seemed blithely unaware of her reined-in-feelings. "That was going to be the surprise!"

"That's quite a surprise," Annie said in clipped tones. "Am I supposed to jump up and down for joy, Ellis?"

He stared at her, puzzled. "What's wrong?" he asked. "I thought you'd be happy about it. It's an honor—it's the greatest opportunity a doctor can possibly have. The finest facilities in the country, unlimited funding . . . it's the chance of a lifetime!"

"Well, in *that* case, congratulations!" Annie snapped. "How foolish of me," she added sarcastically, "to have thought that you might have told me first!"

"I just wasn't thinking straight." Ellis shook his head and chuckled. "I completely forgot about your access to UPI and AP . . . but I don't understand why you're angry, darling."

Annie stared at him, amazed. His surprise was genuine, she thought. Didn't he have any idea what he'd done, what he'd said? She shook her head, staring out at the rain, which was beginning to pound heavily on the deck.

"Ellis," she said, keeping her voice steady, "did you ever stop to think about us?"

"Of course!" Ellis's expression cleared. "Oh, Annie, don't tell me that you actually thought I would leave . . ." He stared at her in sudden dismay. "What a fool I was!" Then a smile broke across his handsome features. "That was the surprise, darling—we'll get married and move there together. They've got the greatest old houses, and there are fantastic renovations being done. You'll love it," he assured her happily.

Annie just stared blankly at him. Married? Moving? He'd planned all that out without so much as bothering to consult her? She shook her head as if to clear it.

"You can't be serious," she said incredulously. "Do you really expect me to simply pick up and leave New Orleans, just like that?" She snapped her fingers.

"Well, it won't be for two months," Ellis assured her. "I've got to finish a project here, and . . ."

"No, Ellis," Annie interrupted, "that's not what I meant at all." The words came out flatly. "I meant, you can't really believe that I'd just give up my career, my friends, everything I've worked so hard to achieve here—just to follow you to a strange city."

"You can get a job there," Ellis said. "There are affiliate stations . . ."

"You simply aren't thinking at all, are you?" Annie asked angrily. "Do you think I got where I am overnight? It's been a struggle for me . . . and I'm finally being rewarded for that struggle! I'm serious about what I do, Ellis. Or were you laboring under the delusion that I was just biding my time, waiting around until Mr. Right would come along and take me away from all this?"

Ellis's eyes darkened. "Annie, you're not being fair," he stated, his voice controlled. "Of course I believe you're serious, *and* I know how good you are at what you do. I'm certainly not asking you to give that up . . ."

"Then what *are* you asking me to do?" Annie snapped.

"I'm asking you to share your life with me," Ellis replied soberly. "What's so terrible about that?"

"Share!" Annie repeated. "You don't know the meaning of the word! You're discounting everything I do! You don't want a partner, Ellis—you just want a yes-man, no, I should say, a yes-*woman*. Someone who'll do whatever you want, whenever you want—someone who'll follow you at a snap of your fingers, who'll never have a thought or decision or goal of her own. How dare you make these kinds of life decisions by yourself and expect me to fall into line?"

"You're being impossible!" Ellis's voice rose angrily. "You know that my work comes first. You've always known that! And I think you're being pretty damned selfish and shortsighted if you can't admit that it's more important for me to be where I can work on advancing medicine than it is for you to stay where you happen to feel safe and accepted in your work!"

"I think that being a doctor has gone to your head," Annie retorted. "You seem to think that you're *God!* Just dismissing my entire life . . ."

"I am *not* dismissing it," Ellis replied through clenched teeth. "But it seems that that's exactly what you're doing to me! Hell, Annie, you said you loved me . . ."

"Does that mean I'm supposed to just relinquish my identity?" Annie broke in sarcastically.

"Dammit, listen to me!" She had never seen Ellis this angry, his handsome features contorted. "I've had to battle you every step of the way—for your trust, your confidence, and for what you claimed was your love. It has *not* been easy!" His gray eyes were stormy. "Now, you want to fight me about this, too—the one thing I thought we could agree on—about meeting me halfway."

"Meeting you halfway means dropping my life and everything I care about?"

"How silly of me," Ellis said coldly. "I just assumed that of all the things you cared about, I was the most important. I guess I was wrong. You don't believe in me—you don't trust me—and I guess you never will."

Annie was stunned by the cold finality of his voice. She stared up at him, confused. But before she could formulate her next words, Ellis continued.

"Maybe you're just not ready to drop all those well-placed barriers, Annie. Maybe you just don't have what it takes to *be* a partner. Although, God knows, I wanted you to. Maybe you really want your life simple, un-cluttered—and uninvolved." He stared inquiringly at her.

"Maybe you're right, Ellis," Annie replied, matching his cold tone of voice. "It certainly seems that you and I have very different goals and expectations...and I guess that just boils down to the fact that we're really unsuited to one another."

The boat rocked suddenly, whipped by a gust of wind. The sky was darkening ominously, and the rainfall, which had gone from light to heavy during their con-versation, was now slanting down in sheets from above. Perfect weather, Annie thought grimly, for a dead-end confrontation.

"It would appear that, for once, you're right." Ellis's voice had ice in it. "I suppose it's better this way. At least we haven't done irrevocable—or legal—damage to each other."

Annie rose, and, bracing herself against the rocking motion of the boat, reached for her purse. "I'm sorry, Ellis," she said formally, "but it *is* better this way. Far better. Well, there's no graceful way to end this con-versation. So I'll just say good bye." She turned to go, half expecting him to stop her.

But he didn't. Annie turned back, and saw that he'd disappeared below deck. Well, she thought, stung by his apparent indifference, there really *wasn't* anything left to say, anyway. Then, squaring her shoulders, she walked away from the *Aurora,* and away from Ellis.

CHAPTER

Eleven

THE WET STREETS and the swish of the windshield wipers kept Annie's concentration on her driving as she headed for her apartment. Once there, she could not fight off the memory of Ellis's bitter words.

Had she finally driven him away with her obstinance, her refusal to compromise—her personal demons? She shook her head unable to sort out all the variables in this situation. It seemed that one minute, they were happily discussing how they would spend the rest of their lives together, and the next minute they were battling to the hilt about how they could even coexist.

Perhaps Ellis was right, she reflected. Perhaps she was so set in her ways, so defensive, so determined not to give in to anything, ever, that she could never change. As Annie pulled off her wet clothes, she envisioned what it would be like to spend the rest of her life the way she had spent the past four years. It wasn't bad she thought—just a bit lonely at times. But, after knowing what it was like to love and be loved by a man like Ellis, how could she ever live like that again?

Impatiently, Annie pulled on dry cords and a heavy sweater. She grabbed a pair of soft leather boots and zipped them up. She hadn't received any messages from

WJNO, but she wanted to be ready, in case she had to dash off to the station. On second thought, she realized, what she really wanted was to talk to someone who would understand all this mess. Annie threw her beeper into her purse, yanked on her trenchcoat and headed impatiently down to her car. Nancy would be at one of her galleries, she thought, and right now, Annie needed a sympathetic ear now more than ever.

Rain was pouring down in sheets as she drove carefully through the flooded streets. It was almost impossible to make out signs, lights, or dividing lines and Anne felt a moment of panic, trapped helpless in the tiny light car. Overcoming her fear, she kept to a careful crawl and heaved a sigh of relief when she saw Nancy's camper parked directly in front of Gallerie Bleau. Through the misty downpour, Annie could see Nancy struggling with heavy wooden shutters, trying to secure them over her large storefront windows.

Pulling the Alfa to the curb, Annie ran through the deluge and joined Nancy as she tried to hold the shutters long enough to latch them.

Annie," Nancy exclaimed with astonishment. "What are you doing out in this mess?"

"Nancy, I have to talk with you," Annie shouted over the din as she held the shutter and Nancy secured it.

"Sure, c'mon in, I'll put on a pot of coffee." Her friend offered, noting the tears welling up in Annie's eyes.

No sooner had they stepped inside and started getting out of their dripping coats, then Annie's beeper went off with a piercing electronic tone. Annie reached inside her purse and shut it off, resenting the interruption of her pressing need to talk with Nancy. "Business first," she said with a frustrated shrug.

"Phone's over there, hon," Nancy replied with a gesture toward her little office in the back. "I'll put on the coffee."

Annie picked up the phone and dialed WJNO, where a weekend secretary answered and put her call immediately through to David. His voice was calm, despite a note of urgency.

"Where are you?" he asked promptly.

"At Nancy's gallery in the Quarter."

"Do you think you can get over here?" David asked dubiously. "Or do you want me to send the van to pick you up?"

"The rain's coming down pretty hard, David, but it'd be quicker if I drove down myself. I should be able to make it to the station all right. Want to tell me what's up?"

"Storm damage. It's really starting to pile up," David said succinctly. "There are several areas that are flooding badly. We should have somebody there to cover it. I'll fill you in when you get here. How long?"

Annie glanced at her watch, trying to estimate how long it would take in this wind and rain to get from the French Quarte to the station. "I'll try for twenty minutes," she said cautiously. "I can't promise, but don't send anyone else. I want to do this story, David."

"You got it," he promised and clicked off the line.

Nancy already had Annie's trenchcoat in her hands as Annie hung up the receiver. While Annie pulled it on, tightening the belt around her waist, Nancy rooted around in her storage closet and emerged with a large black umbrella.

"Here," she said handing it to Annie. "Honestly, I can't figure out how you ever went out today without one."

Annie grinned as her spirits rose with the prospect of an exciting upcoming assignment. "Gotta go," she said, hugging her friend affectionately.

"Any time I can be of help, let me know," Nancy replied with a smile.

Nancy accompanied her to the door, grimacing as she pulled it open and felt a blast of icy air. "You be careful, now," she warned. "I've been through a few of these and they can be really dangerous."

"Don't worry," Annie called as she made a mad dash for her car. "Bye."

Guiding the little sports car at a snail's pace, Annie thought the streets looked like little running rivers. Grimly she realized that the drive to the gallery had been a picnic compared to this. She'd never been in a storm this intense before and she was in awe of this display of nature's overwhelming power.

Annie concentrated on steering the car, trying to keep the light vehicle out of the worst of the flooding. All she needed now, Annie thought morosely, was to have her battery get drenched and have the car stall in some god-forsaken spot where there probably wouldn't be any working phones.

She thought fleetingly of Ellis. If only she hadn't ruined things between them, Annie reflected, chastizing herself. Ellis had been marvelously patient with her— far more than she had been with him. But it was hard to forget the cool, hard look in his eyes when she left the boat.

Well, she reminded herself, there was absolutely nothing she could do about it now. She'd acted like such a fool, she mused. Why had she let her pride and stubbornness get the better of her?

So much for daydreaming, she told herself, as the car

bounced over a rut in the road. What would be would be. Right now, she had to worry about getting herself to the station in one piece. She could barely see ten feet in front of her; the windshield wipers were virtually useless against the torrents of rain which beat against the window. At least she could be grateful there weren't many other cars on the road. Only a fool or a reporter would go out in weather like this.

Annie could see the station lights looming up ahead. Their friendly glow was uplifting and Annie pulled into the underground parking area. As she took her hands away from the wheel, Annie realized that her fingers were stiff and cramped from clenching the steering wheel so hard. She flexed them a few times to get the circulation going and then stretched her legs out of the car. She hadn't been conscious that she'd tensed every muscle in her body trying to maneuver through the dangerous streets but her stiff back and tight neck told the whole story.

Inside the station, there were lots of people milling around. This was definitely not the usual skeleton crew that worked the weekends. As she looked around, it seemed to Annie, that the air was charged with excitement. In fact, she thought, it rarely felt this tense in the newsroom. She headed for David's office without even removing her coat.

"Oh, Miss Carroll, there you are." It was a vaguely familiar girl from the weekend secretarial pool. "Mr. Sommers is waiting for you in the conference room," the girl said with a bit of nervous exhaustion in her voice.

"Thanks," Annie replied with a casual wave and headed down the hall. Inside the conference room, she found David, Rudy, Joe, and Jackson Cahill, along with his own mobile team.

"Annie, we'd begun to think we'd have to send out a search and rescue team for you." David managed a light smile despite his obvious fatigue. "Okay, now that you're here, let's get down to business. I'm sending both of you," he indicated Annie and Cahill, "to different trouble spots. The wind force is already at gale level—well over fifty miles an hour—and it's still rising. The weather guys are a bit baffled. This seems to have come up without any real warning. They're anticipating it getting a lot worse before it gets better. We'll work on translating their technical jargon into layman terms so you can integrate them into your reports. So far so good?"

David looked around and received affirmative nods from his reporters. "Okay," he continued, pointing to a large map he'd spread out on the center of the conference table, "these are the spots which are having some real problems. Jackson, let's take your team first."

Annie watched with interest as David detailed the location and its problems. Jackson and his team were to be sure to cover the real possibility of a failure in the large power plant in the area. She found a moment to throw a quick smile to Joe and Rudy, who, as usual, seemed to be taking the whole business in stride.

"Okay, Annie, now you." David pointed to a suburban area outside New Orleans proper, across the Pearl River. "There's a history of storm damage in this area," he told her. "The flooding is always bad and it's basically a residential area, so there's probably a lot of citizens up to their necks in water. The place is single-family dwellings, schools, churches, that sort of thing. Got it?"

"No problem," Annie assured him. "Is this the bridge we need to take?" she asked, indicating the spot on the map with her index finger.

"That's it," David replied. "Rudy, Joe, any questions?"

"Nope," Rudy said and Joe shook his head in agreement.

"I know the area," Joe added. "Got a brother-in-law who lives out that way."

"Great," David said briskly. "Let's get going. All of you be careful. I don't want any casualties from the WJNO teams. We'll have enough headlines without you people adding your own names to the list. Got it?"

"Can we get hazardous duty pay?" Jackson joked. David relaxed and smiled.

"I doubt it," he said, "but I meant what I said about being careful."

"Yes, boss!" Annie saluted him cheerfully and got up. "Come on you guys, let's get going." She could feel the adrenaline beginning to rush through her system as she considered going out in the storm and what she might find there.

"Hey," Joe protested jokingly, "we were ready an hour ago!"

"Don't give me that," Annie grinned back at him. "My beeper hadn't even gone off then."

"Stop squabbling," Rudy interjected. "Let's go fill a couple of thermoses with hot coffee and get some sandwiches to take with us. Somehow I've got the feeling that we're not going to find an awful lot of all-night restaurants open."

They all piled out of the conference room and set about getting these last supplies together for the trip. She saw Rudy toss a bottle of bourbon into the knapsack with the rest of the supplies and Annie couldn't help but smile. It was definitely going to be a long night.

CHAPTER
Twelve

ANNIE STARED OUT the passenger window of the van, awestruck by the fury of the storm. Beside her, Joe fought the wheel against the gusts of wind that buffeted the heavy vehicle, nearly blowing it off the road at times. All around them cars were stalled and streets were flooded. Annie saw a young woman and child hurrying through the slashing rain and silently prayed the two would make it home all right.

The drive was extremely risky in such weather, but then, she reflected, that's what the job was all about. Joe had both the CB and the police scanner on, and he changed course several times as reports came on alerting them to roads that were blocked or no longer navigable.

"If this wind keeps up, we'll have a hurricane on our hands for sure," Joe commented.

"Here, Annie get into these. That coat of yours won't be worth a damn once we get outside into this." Rudy's voice was strictly no nonsense as he handed her a heavy yellow rain slicker and a pair of high rubber boots.

"You think we'll be able to get through?" Annie asked as she obeyed Rudy, slipping the boots over her own and squirming into the raincoat.

"Don't rightly know, Annie," Joe replied, squinting

through the clouded windshield. "This looks pretty bad."

"I was in a big one, like this, maybe twenty years ago," Rudy reflected. "I was just a kid, but I remember being blown so hard that I couldn't keep my feet. If I hadn't been able to grab onto a tree and hang on until my daddy got to me . . . Well, you'd be having somebody else recording your sound is all I can say." A screaming police siren drowned out any further words.

Joe had the van headed on a course parallel to the mighty Mississippi and Annie could barely make out muddy brown water beginning to crest over its banks— a sure sign of impending disaster for the city. Even the van's powerful heater couldn't stop the chills that Annie felt as she witnessed the storm's growing power. This was by far the most demanding assignment she'd ever had and, secretly, Annie hoped she'd prove equal to the task of covering the event.

For a while, no one said anything as Joe guided the van resolutely through the storm. The only sound was the rain pelting the steel roof of the heavy vehicle and, as Annie stared out the clouded windows, her thoughts turned inward.

Had she really made a mess of things? Had she driven Ellis off forever? As Annie's eyes traced the rivulets that coursed down the windows, she considered Ellis's proposal once again. There was no mistaking his sincerity when he proclaimed his love for her; Annie knew that for sure. But how could she just pack up and leave her job, her friends, everything she cared about behind? Nancy and Kevin were like family to her and the news station was like a second home. Sure, she had told Ellis to forget about marriage. But what would she really do without him? Annie wondered as her hands unconsciously twisted the note pad on her lap.

Despite everything, Annie loved him; there was no denying it. But her subconscious defenses had intervened like a warning bell and the fear that her life was being manipulated beyond her control, beyond her wishes, had been too strong to suppress.

Thinking back on Ellis's words, Annie could almost hear his husky voice saying that she had to start believing in someone sometime and that someone should be Ellis. She knew she couldn't go around for the rest of her life unable to trust someone. And, after all, it wasn't as if Ellis asked her to give up her career or change her values and way of life.

The van bucked through a deep puddle, sending up a spray of water on either side. But the break in her thoughts was only momentary as Annie's self-scrutiny continued.

For the first time she considered what it would be like if the shoe were on the other foot. What if it was she who had the chance of a big job, perhaps in New York, where the network headquarters were located. And what if Ellis was the one with the more flexible profession, something that didn't require a geographically fixed research facility, such as an opthamologist. After swearing her undying love for him what would her reaction be if he said *no*, he couldn't leave the town where he had settled, even though he could work just as effectively in New York. Of course she'd be upset, perhaps to the point of thinking that he didn't love her enough to follow her. Is that what he was thinking of her now—that she didn't love him enough? It's not true! She shouted inwardly. Of course she loved him, more than she ever could imagine. Everything inside Annie suddenly cried out that she loved Ellis Greystone.

She couldn't let him believe otherwise, Annie realized. He'd asked her to marry him and, like a fool, she turned him down. Tears of frustration welled up in Annie's eyes and she wondered what Ellis must think. If only she could have let him know how deeply she felt for him before he went to Baltimore. Sure he'd assumed she'd move with him, changing all her well thought out plans. But it was a small price to pay, Annie realized, if it meant spending the rest of her life with the man she loved. It all seemed so clear. There was room in her life to have Ellis. She hoped it wasn't too late. If he'd still have her, she'd marry him, no matter what he asked in return.

A quick bright flash illuminated the entire van and Annie saw a wicked finger of lightning streak out of the sky and strike a tall wooden telephone pole. A billowing puff of smoke followed and severed electrical wires cascaded down to the ground. Then the upper portion of the pole toppled into the street and Joe slammed his foot hard on the brake to bring the van to a sliding stop just inches from the dancing, sparking wires and charred wooden debris.

"God! That was close," Joe blurted, as he paused, trying to catch his breath.

"One more incident like that and we'll have to call it a day," Rudy agreed. "If," he added grimly, "we're still able."

The police scanner continued to squawk over the crew's chatter, but even without the bulletins, it was all too evident that the storm's intensity was increasing. Again and again, fingers of lightening streaked out of a nearly pitch-black sky, followed by rolling, cracking thunder. The rain continued to pour down; drops were no longer even discernible, only tremendous sheets of water which slammed into the van and made Annie won-

der how this machine, let alone frail humans, could withstand the onslaught. But Joe managed to nurse the vehicle
along, and they slowly turned and left the city behind,
inching their way towards the suburbs.

As they neared their destination, reports came over
the scanner indicating that the only bridge connecting the
isolated township to the city was in jeopardy. If the water
level rose much more, the bridge might even go down.
Joe's face was set in grim determination, and Annie could
see that he planned to get there in time to cross over.
Annie jotted down some notes, describing the house-
lined streets around them, and the water which was already lapping at some front doors.

Up ahead, she could just barely make out a swirl of
flashing red lights. In between ineffectual swipes of the
windshield wipers, she saw several police cars positioned
near the gray, hulking girders of a two-lane bridge. As
they got nearer, Annie could see that state troopers were
stopping cars and turning people around, and she
groaned. Joe slowed the van to a crawl as they reached
the slickered trooper who was directing traffic.

Joe rolled to a stop and lowered his window as the
trooper yelled over the howling wind, "Sorry folks, this
is the end of the line. That bridge is gonna go any
minute."

Annie held her press credentials out to the officer.
"We're on assignment for WJNO, officer, and we've got
a tyrant of a news director who won't let us come back
without a story. Surely you can make an exception,"
Annie wheedled.

"I'd like to help, ma'am, but this truck of yours must
weigh near a ton and that bridge may not be able to take
it," the trooper said apologetically. "Besides, tyrant or
not, I'm sure he'd rather have his crew alive!"

A loud commotion erupted behind them, and the trooper turned his attention to the pickup behind them, and its driver, a young man who was being restrained by two other officers. The man's protests pierced the howling cacophony of wind, rain, and sirens, and Annie could just make out that he lived across the river, and was desperate to get to his family on the other side.

The officer at their window yelled at Joe, "Go on, get this thing turned around . . . now!" and moved off to assist in the restraint of the impassioned young man.

Annie, Joe, and Rudy exchanged glances. "Go for it," Annie said.

Joe rolled up the window and floored the van. It was too quick and unexpected a move for the officers to react, and before they knew it, the van had barreled past the blockade and onto the bridge. Then Joe immediately cut the speed, and they proceeded cautiously over the shaky structure.

Annie bit into her knuckle as she looked over the side and saw the river, formerly calm and shallow, now raging a scant few feet below them. The bridge gave a sudden lurch, and her stomach knotted in fear as the vehicle seemed to drop a full foot. She closed her eyes and prayed they'd make it to the other side, then opened them again, afraid she'd miss something important.

But the bridge held, and, as they emerged onto the far shore, the three of them breathed a collective sigh of relief. Gazing back at the river, Annie was amazed at the depth of the raging torrent of debris-filled water: it was starting to wash over the concrete levees that normally kept the town from flooding. But the rain continued to pour down, swelling the little river, and it seemed to be only a matter of time before the barriers gave way.

Reading her mind, Rudy suggested they move to

higher, safer ground, then saw yet another trooper flagging them down. Unable to move at more than a crawl through the overflowing streets, Joe once again stopped the van and rolled his window down.

"That was a damned foolish thing to do," the trooper began but before any of them could reply, he continued, "There's a first-aid station set up over at the high school. You all had better head on over that way, unless you wanna have this thing float away with you."

Annie leaned across to the driver's window. "Officer, I'm..."

"Anne Caroll," he finished for her, squinting in recognition. "Yes, ma'am. What can I do for you?"

Rudy promptly passed the compact portable camera up to Joe and thrust out the microphone. As Joe focused in on the officer, Annie asked, "How bad is the situation here, Officer?..."

"Bennett, ma'am, Sergeant Jerry Bennett. It's pretty bad right now. The streets are completely flooded. You can see for yourself, water level's ranging from two feet up to people's rooflines in the lower areas. It's almost impossible for rescue vehicles to get through, and most of the power's out except for the emergency generator at the high school. We're tryin' to evacuate as many people as possible over that way."

"What's the biggest danger here?" Annie continued.

"Well, the Red Cross is setting up cots and blankets and food at the gym, but a lot of folks are stranded. *That's* where the biggest problem lies, gettin' those people to safety. But, as you can see, it isn't going to be easy." He pointed toward a family stranded on the rooftop of a small frame house.

"Get that, Joe," Annie said, and Joe swung his camera in a short pan past the officer.

"What about you, Sergeant Bennett. Do you have family here?" Annie asked, remembering David's "human interest" dictum.

"Yes, ma'am, I do...my wife and two boys. I'm pretty sure they're at the school by now, but it looks like it'll be some time before I get to see them."

From behind them came the loud groaning of metal and concrete, and the officer backed away from the van, peering through the storm in the direction of the noise. Annie and her crew quickly scrambled out of the van in time to see the bridge begin to give way.

It was an awesome sight, and Annie stared, mesmerized, as the huge mass began to slump and sway. It took only moments for the entire structure to become useless to any more traffic. A few minutes ago, they had been on that bridge, Annie thought with a shudder. Now, it was reduced to broken chunks of concrete and a few girders still sticking up above the raging torrent of muddy water. Another rumbling sound filled the air, and Rudy pointed to the concrete levee cracking, crumbling, and finally bursting forth with a monstrous waterfall.

Annie realized they'd better get out of the way fast. But when she looked around for Rudy and Joe, she saw them standing fast, filming and recording the massive downpour of water from the broken levee. Running over to them, she grabbed Joe by the collar and yanked Rudy's headphones off. "Come on, you guys," she yelled over the wind, "let's get out of here, over to the high school!"

Joe grinned. "Just gettin' some good footage for you, boss," he shouted back. Then the three of them beat a hasty retreat to the van, piling in and driving off just as the tide swelled up to the doorjams.

They drove carefully past stalled cars, uprooted trees, and churning debris. Annie cried out in horror as she saw a large dog, his collar caught on the branch of a fallen tree, struggling to keep his head above water. His frantic barks were becoming garbled as the water rose close to his mouth.

"Joe, pull over!" Annie said impulsively, and he promptly did as she wished.

Rudy quickly slid the van's side door open and reaching out, grabbed the shaggy mutt's collar. "It's okay, boy, just . . . one . . . more . . . minute and . . . Gotcha!"

To Annie's relief, Rudy hauled the frightened animal into the van. He promptly coughed up a lot of water, barked his thanks, and wiggled his soaking body, sending a shower around the interior of the van. Tension eased, all three of them laughed heartily.

As they approached the high school, stragglers carrying bags, or just in the clothes on their backs, were entering the building. The gym was on a slight rise, high enough to remain safe from the swelling waters, and, relieved to be out of danger, Annie, the crew, and their new-found canine friend tramped wearily into the shelter.

Along one wall were perhaps three dozen cots, where several exhausted families were resting and assessing their losses. Against another wall, Red Cross volunteers were handing out blankets and serving steaming soup to the homeless families, and to fatigued troopers. A few other tables were set up, away from the food and cots, and it was here that Annie could see the greatest toll the storm had taken. Three overtaxed nurses and one lone fireman were trying to tend to the injured. A little boy held back his tears as his mother cradles his head and the fireman put makeshift splints around his badly fractured leg. One woman had fainted, and several other people waited for attention to cuts, breaks, and other injuries. It was a distressing sight, and Annie's reaction was compassionate as she saw these flood victims waiting stoically while the understaffed medical crew worked feverishly. Too many people had suffered already from this storm's fury, and it was up to her to make sure that their plight was conveyed to the rest of the country.

"All right, Rudy, Joe, this isn't exactly pretty," she said grimly. "We've got to get as much of it on film as possible, okay?"

The directive was barely out of her mouth before her crew began surveying the situation, readying their gear. Annie turned her attention to an elderly couple who'd had the roof to their home literally ripped off by the gale-force winds, when she heard the commotion coming from the entrance to the gym.

"What the hell does that fool think he's *doing?*" A disbelieving deputy blurted the words as he pointed out something to his tired partner. "He must be crazy to try something like that!"

Annie hurried over to see what was causing all the furor. "What's happening, officer?" she asked, following the line of his pointing finger.

"There's a guy trying to cross the downed bridge. He's going to drown, for sure!"

Annie squinted in an effort to see through the blinding swirl of wind and water. It appeared that there was a figure trying to cross the twisted ruins of the bridge, and Annie thought of the young man in the pickup who'd been restrained while she and the WJNO van ran the blockade. She could barely make out the man, who was having a difficult time negotiating the precarious mass of wreckage. Annie began to feel a peculiar sense of dread as she watched the dangerous crossing; she couldn't make out any distinct features at this distance, but the movements were familiar. Adrenaline rushed through her body, and she scanned the gym quickly.

"Joe, quick! Bring the camera," she called, and the cameraman hustled over. "Point it at the bridge and let me look through the viewfinder, will you?"

Joe held the instrument, and its rubber eye cup up to Annie, and placed her hands on the ring surrounding the telephoto lens. "Here," he explained, "this racks focus and this extends focal length—zoom in or out."

Annie centered the viewfinder crosshairs on the man and brought his image closer, then twisted the focus ring until he was no longer a blur. His black hair was flying in the wind as he forced his way through the slanted sheets of rain. He staggered, reached out a hand, grabbed a protruding beam to steady himself and turned full face in her direction.

"Ellis!" Annie gasped. She kept her eyes glued to his image as, features contorted in determination, he fought his way across. Behind him, a pair of state troopers called out, urging him back, but he didn't seem to hear them. Halfway across, he lost his footing and nearly fell into the raging flood beneath him; but he righted himself and continued on. With his every step, Annie became more distraught. Only a man in superb physical condition could even contemplate attempting such a dangerous feat, she knew; but even Ellis' prowess might not match the tempest that tore at him. Finally, unable to contain her fears, she thrust the camera back at Joe and rushed out of the gym, down toward the bridge.

The dog they'd saved bounded after her, barking happily, and together they sloshed through the water toward the bridge. Annie's breathing came in gasps as she strained against the mud sucking at her feet. Although the storm continued unabated, the torrent from the levee had slowed enough to allow her to approach the banks.

About twenty yards from the bridge, Annie saw that he was nearly across. And, looking ahead, Ellis recognized her and broke into a smile. They came closer and closer until, finally, he had one last step to go. With a jump, he alighted next to her. Annie stared at his muddied face, and, thanking God that he was alive, fell into his arms.

"Ellis, you must be mad. What made you do it? You could have been killed!" Annie's eyes were huge with panic and relief.

"It's all right, Annie, it was easier than it looked." Ellis made light of the journey, in an attempt to allay her fears. "Besides, when David told me where you were, I thought, well . . . I just wanted to reach you."

They stared at each other, drenched and cold, the dog dancing circles around them, barking excitedly.

"First things first," Annie said firmly. "You've got to get dry and you need something hot to drink. Come on, there's an aide station set up in the high school gym. The crew's there now." As they struggled up the hill together, Annie turned to him for a moment. "I guess your flight was grounded?" she asked tentatively.

"And I'm glad it was. So much has happened since I saw you . . . I've got a million things to tell you."

Before he could continue, the dog gave a howl and bounded off toward the gym, where a small boy stood with his mother. The boy's face lit up and he ran toward the dog, who whimpered in delight. Annie guessed that her canine friend had been reunited with his master, and she smiled.

"It's kind of a long story," Ellis began. But by now, they were inside the gym, and Ellis stopped speaking as he looked around, his face registering deep concern as he assessed the situation. "And it'll have to wait," he said firmly to Annie. "Things look bad here."

He removed his arm from Annie's shoulder and strode

to the area of the gym where the fireman and a few nurses were struggling to keep pace with the swelling numbers of the injured.

"What's the situation here, Captain?" Ellis asked.

"I'm not a captain," the fireman replied wearily as he bandaged an elderly woman's cut forehead, "and you can see for yourself how bad it is. There are at least fifty people who need medical attention, and more coming in, every minute. Unless you're an emergency case, please wait over by the bleachers. We'll get to you as soon as we can."

Annie saw Ellis smile in sympathy. "It's okay, I'm not hurt. I'm a physician. Can I lend a hand?"

The fireman lifted his head, looking relieved. "You bet we can use your help. The local doctor is stranded on the other side of the river, and with all the flooding on the roads, it's going to be a while before we get any relief medical help here."

"Why don't you take a break," Ellis suggested. "Get something to eat, and grab an hour's sleep. I can keep it under control." He unslung a small backpack and withdrew his black medical bag. "Annie," he called, "you mind alternating with the nurses for a bit? They've got to get some rest before they drop. And I've got a feeling it's going to get worse before it gets better."

"No problem," Annie replied promptly. "Rudy, Joe, get over here, will you?" she beckoned. Turning back to Ellis she asked, "What can we do?"

"For starters, let's see if we can get the injured organized. Get the serious ones up front to me now, then try to line people up according to the extent of their problems. Oh, and ask around, see if anybody has any prescription pain killers. I have a feeling I don't have nearly enough in my bag."

Working together, they soon had things well organized, and Annie was pleasantly surprised to see such a prominent surgeon responding to the state of emergency with a manner befitting a personable country doctor. Surgeons in general had reputations as egocentric and vain, but Ellis was proving quite the opposite. She could see him continue to respond with genuine humanity as the number of patients grew, and their wails of pain and discomfort grew throughout the cavernous gym. It didn't seem to bother him that patients irrationally blamed *him* for the pain even while he worked valiantly to ease it. And his authoritative presence was like a beacon to the tired volunteers. Despite fatigue, sore feet, and hours without relief, they seemed to draw new energy from working with this tireless professional.

Finished with her relief work for the moment, Annie turned her attention to the homeless people seeking refuge from the storm in this makeshift shelter. It appeared that many of the residents from this isolated community were being reunited with their families, trying to assess the toll the storm was taking on their lives. Farmers, businessmen, troopers, kids, teachers, housewives—all shared soup side by side, attempting to comfort one another. The sight of this gathering of humanity huddled beneath a communal roof renewed Annie's determination to accurately portray as much of their recent, terrible experience as she could. It was time for her to get to her assignment.

As if they were on the same wavelength, Annie saw Joe loading his camera with a fresh roll of film; and Rudy was already waiting with the recorder. The trio converged, plotting the strategy of their coverage. Since they'd be unable to get anything across live, they would just film as much as they wanted. Then, as soon as the storm broke, they would get the material back to the station for immediate editing and broadcast.

The high windows that extended nearly to the rafters of the tall building were now totally black. Looking at her watch, Annie was surprised to see that they were already well into the night. There seemed to be no let up in sight, as rain continued to pelt the building, and glass rumbled from the pressure of the winds. They would probably be safe here, Annie surmised, but there was no doubt that they were all bound to be together for the rest of the night.

"We might as well make the best of it," she said philosophically to the crew. "This is an opportunity to talk to people from all walks of life—to get the story from every angle. David wanted human interest, well, he's going to get it!"

Joe and Rudy nodded in agreement, and Annie felt her spirits lift, as determination and purpose fueled her on. She began to interview people at random, acquiring a variety of emotion-packed stories.

A barber told of sandbagging the entrance to his shop, only to have the flood waters creep relentlessly higher and higher, until the shop was flooded. He'd had to abandon everything to get himself and his family to the shelter.

The mayor, a short, balding man, described his efforts to summon authorities and to organize rescue efforts. Despite the destruction caused by the flood, he was still hopeful about the future. Annie's ability to convey sympathy brought out the determination in the man. His constituents had survived the tragedy, and, despite devastating losses, they would begin to rebuild their little town just as soon as the storm ended.

Rudy pointed to a trooper in a yellow slicker, surrounded by a woman and two little boys. Annie recognized Jerry Bennett, the officer they'd talked to just after crossing the bridge. Annie talked with him again now, happily reunited with his family. He described his efforts to make sure that there were no residents left stranded on rooftops, or caught in stalled autos. By the time he'd been relieved, Bennett had been so exhausted that he nearly missed his wife and kids as he'd staggered into the gym. Just then, the officer's youngest son handed his father a mug of hot soup. As the weary man took the cup, he was unable to restrain his emotions any longer, and he hugged the boy tearfully to his chest. Annie made sure Joe got it all on film: the moment was too precious to lose.

She saw Ellis and the nurses laboring into the night, pictures of total dedication. All around her, it seemed, people were calling on their last, best reserves of energy to deal with this crisis. And Annie and her crew also worked into the night, gaining a measure of strength from the people around them, sharing the strife and compassion in the face of nature's awesome fury.

When Joe went to the van for more film, Annie slumped on the bleachers, holding a cup of coffee, trying to organize her thoughts on the wealth of human interest stories they were recording. Brushing strands of disheveled hair from her brow, she put her pencil to the pad and concentrated on how best to convey the events of the night. She considered several people they'd interviewed, and made some preliminary notes on how to structure and edit this incredible story.

It had to have a solid point of view, and it was from her perspective that the rest of the country would see this event. Looking wearily around her, Annie felt she owed it to these brave survivors to get their story across with all the impact, drama, and tragedy that was inherent in it.

Like a marathon runner, gaining a second wind just when he feels ready to drop, Annie felt a renewed energy for the task at hand. This was by far the most demanding assignment she'd ever had, and she was gladly rising to the challenge, putting her skills to their most difficult test. She was no longer a novice in any sense of the word, in awe of the news business or of its veteran reporters. Now she was the veteran pursuing her story. And it was going to be a damned good one!

She glanced over at Ellis, still working with his original fervor, although the lines of fatigue were evident on his face. Throughout this ordeal, he'd retained his composure and his warmth, treating every patient as if they were the most important person in the world. He looked up from his makeshift examination table and caught Annie's eyes on him. An unspoken communication conveyed their mutual respect, as well as something more intimate. Annie smiled as Ellis's attention was diverted to a trooper with a broken wrist.

There was no mistaking his dedication to his profession, for his genius. She could understand his need to go to Baltimore and take advantage of the best facilities available. It was beyond the limits of her imagination to think what he might do for mankind, given the greatest resources medical science had to offer.

Neither was there any question of her own dedication to *her* profession; and the hard-earned position she held at WJNO was nothing to be taken lightly. But now, she realized, was not the place so much as the situation that a good reporter responded to. There were few doubts left: Annie felt capable of succeeding anywhere now. There would be other disasters and other major events to cover in another city. She could do just as well anywhere. And, if she was with Ellis, it wouldn't matter where they were. Now, more than ever, she was determined to tell him.

"Annie, I've been listening to the broadcast in the

van," Joe said as he laid down two freshly loaded magazines and settled onto the bleacher beside her and the dozing Rudy. "They say the winds have died down a bit, and the storm is passing back into the Gulf. This has been declared a disaster area, and the governor's called out the National Guard. But the roads are still flooded, and it'll be some time before they get here. Oh, and people are starting to respond: the Red Cross has had calls from people wanting to donate food and clothing, even a rancher who offered his horses to tow out any stalled rescue vehicles. Incredible," Joe repressed a yawn.

"Well, then, we've still got some work to do. You guys feel up to stretching your legs and getting a few more interviews?" Annie asked, nudging Rudy awake.

They continued to work through the night, drinking dozens of cups of coffee. Annie and Ellis barely exchanged words, but she felt like they were working together every step of the way.

The rain finally let up a bit, and a few lighter streaks of gray began to filter through the windows of the gym. A quick glance at her watch confirmed that morning had nearly arrived. With her last bit of energy, Annie stared into Joe's camera, and with Rudy's machine rolling down to the last few feet of tape, she wrapped the report with, "From disaster headquarters, this is Anne Carroll, reporting for WJNO." Then the three of them breathed a collective sigh of relief.

"Let's wrap it. I think we've earned a nap," Annie said, leading the way to the bleachers.

Gray light continued to waver through the windows, lightening the spirits of the tired survivors.

"Quite a night, huh, Carroll?"

Annie turned to see Ellis, stretched out next to her, his long legs resting on the bleacher row in front of them.

"I knew doctors drew late hours sometimes, but this is something else," Annie smiled wearily. "You were incredible."

"You weren't so bad yourself," Ellis replied as he leaned over and placed a quick kiss on the corner of her mouth. Then, with a sigh, he leaned back, and Annie put her head on his shoulder. In the distance, she could hear the faint sounds of engines. They were followed by the steady *whump whump whump* of heavy rescue helicopters beating the air. Annie relaxed, realizing that the National Guard was finally arriving on the scene. They'd made it through the night and the storm, the worst was over. She lifted her head to tell Ellis, but he was sound asleep. Smiling to herself, Annie succumbed to her own fatigue; and, leaning against Ellis's chest, which rose and fell in a steady, comforting rhythm, she too drifted off.

CHAPTER

Thirteen

THE ARRIVAL OF the fresh, energetic National Guard troops, carrying desperately needed supplies lifted a great burden from the shoulders of those who had struggled side by side throughout the long night. Waking from her brief nap, Annie was relieved to see a semblance of order and new hope being brought to the shelter. She looked up and thought she could detect a glimmer of dim sunlight coming through the high, narrow windows of the gym. Was it really possible? she wondered. It had seemed as if the night and the storm would never end.

Annie closed her eyes for a moment, willing some energy back into her own fatigued mind and body. When she opened them again, she was looking straight into Ellis's gray gaze. She gave him a small, tentative smile. Annie knew she could no longer put off what she had to say to him. There were no more emergency cases that required his attention, her broadcast was over, and they were here, together. It was now or never.

As if he could read her mind, Ellis held out his hand. "Let's go see what the outside world looks like," he suggested casually.

Accepting the offer, Annie strolled out of the gym with him, admiring his incredible reserves of energy. He looked hardly the worse for his grueling trip across the river or for an entire night spent tending to emergency victims. Then her attention was diverted.

"Oh, no," Annie gasped, looking around in the daylight at the damage the riverfront community had sustained.

There was debris everywhere: pieces of homes and bits of splintered furniture still floating downstream in the muddy, swollen river; entire toppled trees, bereft of leaves, and smaller limbs which lay on the shore and drifted in the water. She shook her head in disbelief as she saw what had been an entire garage door pass by.

"It's amazing what Nature can do, isn't it," Ellis remarked quietly. "It pays not to forget just how powerful she really is."

"It was my first hurricane," Annie ventured timidly. She felt shy, uncertain about how to approach Ellis now. Even though he was being friendly, her hand in his felt more like a gesture of comraderie—something born of fighting the terrible storm together—than a gesture of love.

"Yes, that's right," Ellis mused. He looked down at her, his eyes serious. "And does it change your feelings about New Orleans?" he asked, a slight smile on his lips.

Annie took a deep breath. "No," she replied firmly. "I guess I'll always love New Orleans—in all her moods. But . . ."

"But what?" he cut in sharply.

"Ellis, I . . . I've . . . Oh, why can't I ever talk when it's important?" Annie bit her lip, vexed, then hurried on. "I have something to tell you, and, well, please don't interrupt me, because I just have to get it out." She stared down at the muddied ground for a moment, gathering her thoughts, and hoping silently that he wouldn't laugh, or worse, reject her. She looked up at him again.

"I've been doing some serious thinking, Ellis. About us—about priorities and needs, and, well, I just want you to know that I love you—more than anything in the world." Annie felt her cheeks flush and she held her hand up to stop him from saying anything yet. "I love you," she repeated, "and I need you. And," she gazed at him, still unable to read the expression on his face, "if you still want me, I'll move to Baltimore with you."

"Do you really mean that?" Ellis asked, raising one eyebrow doubtfully.

Oh, no, Annie thought, I've ruined it. I've finally messed things up beyond all repair. But she couldn't give up now.

"I've never been as serious about anything in my life," she said quietly.

"My God, you really *do* mean it!" Ellis exclaimed wonderingly. "Why the change, all of a sudden?"

Was he really going to make her go through it all? she thought miserably. Well, there was no turning back now—she'd play this final scene out. And she had no one but herself to blame for the outcome.

"I told you," she replied softly, "I love you. I guess I finally realized that nothing's more important than that." Unable to look at him any longer, she stared down at the ground unhappily.

"Well, Ms. Carroll, I have some news for you, too," Ellis announced, tilting her head up and forcing her to look at him. "You're not going to Baltimore."

Her heart plummeted. He really didn't want her any more. But, as she attempted to pull away from his demanding gaze, Ellis smiled.

"Don't look at me that way, Annie," he said. "All I meant was that we're going to be able to stay in New

Orleans after all—that's what I crossed the damned river to tell you!"

"What . . . What do you mean?" she asked weakly.

"I turned down the job at Johns Hopkins. Maybe I'm a fool for doing it, but I guess that's the effect you have on me. Annie, the thought of losing you was too much to endure. I figured what good was it to have only half of what I wanted. No, make that less than half. Darling, you're the most important thing in my life. It took the shock of almost losing you for me to finally realize it."

Annie's heart began beating wildly as Ellis made his proclamation. Nothing could have been more welcome to her ears than to hear this.

A mist filled her eyes and a warmth flooded through her as she realized that the man she loved was making the ultimate sacrifice for her. "Ellis, you mean you're giving up your research plans?"

A smile flickered across his lips. "Well, maybe temporarily. I did a lot of thinking about it and you know what, there's no reason I can't continue my research here in town. It may take a while, but I've got some people in high places on my side. It'll take a lot of cash to do it, but just maybe I can get a new research wing built on the Tulane Medical building. Senator Jaynes should go for it, especially if it will carry his name. After all," he said, a spark lighting his slate eyes, "I did save the old boy's life. Besides, once I convince him of the political mileage he can get out of it, I wouldn't be surprised if he endowed the whole thing to the university. He's already said how much of a kick he got out of being the first human guinea pig for my new technique. But even if he doesn't go for it, Annie, I can get funding somewhere, and in the meantime, I'll be here, with you."

Barely able to see his warm smile through her tear

filled eyes, Annie managed, "You're really staying?"

"We're staying," Ellis corrected. "I'll still play doctor, you're going to continue as the rising star of WJNO—and, we're going to be married as soon as possible. Got it?"

Annie nodded as her emotions raced.

"Annie darling, you don't know how much it meant to me to hear you say that you'd have gone to Baltimore with me. Are all the barriers really gone?" Ellis grazed her soft neck with his mouth, sending a shiver of excitement through her tired body.

Annie pressed herself close to him. "They really are," she assured him in a muted tone, gesturing toward the river. "As surely as the levee and the bridge, they're gone. I'm yours, Ellis—you're all I'll ever want," she declared resolutely. "I'll never jump to conclusions or be stubborn again."

Ellis threw back his head and laughed. "I wish there was a preacher here this minute," he exclaimed, "so I could get that on record—and be married with the 'obey' still in the ceremony."

"Obey?" Annie echoed doubtfully, her eyebrows raised. Then she caught his amused look and joined in the laughter. "Okay," she said, "I see what you mean. No rash promises. But, oh, Ellis, I *do* love you!"

"Next week," he said solemnly.

"What?" Annie shook her head, confused.

"Three days to get the license and no time for you to change your mind, Anne Carroll. You and I were meant to be together and if this wasn't such a messy and public place, I'd prove it to you this minute." He bent to kiss her, sending a wave of desire flooding through her. "Maybe we can get one of those helicopters to airlift us back to town." He grinned wickedly down at her. "I think a long hot bath and a bottle of champagne are in order. How about you, darling?"

"Oh, yes," Annie whispered.

"Mmm, good." Ellis bent to kiss her again. "That's what I wanted to hear from the moment I laid eyes on you. Yes, yes, and yes again. It's all so easy, you stubborn lady. Like I told you before—you're mine, and I intend to take very good care of you. Forever. All you ever had to do was say yes."

All their words were swept away as they fell into each other's arms, locked in an eternal embrace. From somewhere in the distance, the faint sounds of melodic jazz seemed to filter through the air, keeping time to the beating of their hearts . . . and the rest of the world simply disappeared.

Second Chance at Love

All of the above titles are $1.75 per copy

WHAT READERS SAY ABOUT
SECOND CHANCE AT LOVE

"SECOND CHANCE AT LOVE is fantastic."
—*J. L., Greenville, South Carolina**

"SECOND CHANCE AT LOVE has all the romance of the big novels."
—*L. W., Oak Grove, Missouri**

"You deserve a standing ovation!"
—*S. C., Birch Run, Michigan**

"Thank you for putting out this type of story. Love and passion have no time limits. I look forward to more of these good books."
—*E. G., Huntsville, Alabama**

"Thank you for your excellent series of books. Our book stores receive their monthly selections between the second and third week of every month. Please believe me when I say they have a frantic female calling them every day until they get your books in."
—*C. Y., Sacramento, California**

"I have become addicted to the SECOND CHANCE AT LOVE books...You can be very proud of these books....I look forward to them each month."
—*D. A., Floral City, Florida**

"I have enjoyed every one of your SECOND CHANCE AT LOVE books. Reading them is like eating potato chips, once you start you just can't stop."
—*L. S., Kenosha, Wisconsin**

"I consider your SECOND CHANCE AT LOVE books the best on the market."
—*D. S., Redmond, Washington**

*Names and addresses available upon request